BUILD

UNIVERSES

Anthony Gimpel

Emil Finch

europe books

© 2021 **Europe Books**| London
www.europebooks.co.uk | info@europebooks.co.uk

ISBN 979-12-201-1613-8
First edition: November 2021

Distribution for the United Kingdom: **Vine House Distribution ltd**

Printed for Italy by *Rotomail Italia S.p.A. - Vignate (MI)*
Stampato presso *Rotomail Italia S.p.A. - Vignate (MI)*

Emil Finch

and yes I said yes I will yes

Chapter 1
A CONVERSATION
In a Dining Room
You & D

There is blood in the air, fine red droplets gathering speed. Bright, freshly drawn from a gaping wound. Echoes of the past.

You know she's there, you can hear her all the time, whispering words. From the time when there were no words, only feelings, tears, smiles, food, soggy pants, and hugs that never came. There you are scrabbling at the pile with your long thin bony fingers. Your nails are worn short. Sacks in the attic, boxes in the cellar. Mould. Something is recognised, the shape is not lost. Beneath the grime. Booting bits out of the way. Careful, you might have something there. Examine all before discarding. Scrape off the dirt, the shit, squalor of age, with the piss making all of it runny. Digging in the dung heaps. Filthy job but someone has to do it.

Why you?

What do you see there in the dirt? Tucked away, old memories, thrown off, hidden beneath the shopping and the cooking, weeds in the garden, work, mow the lawn, cup of coffee, breakfast, do the dishes, wash the floor, peel potatoes, sign cheques, make love, polish shoes. Tumbled in, pretend forgotten, not gone. Live, eat, sleep, love, work, fuck, shit and die. It's all still there.

She loved you, set you down to lie in a cosy world of blankets and pillows and rubber sheets. She picked you up and held you tight before leaving you to the emptiness

9

of your gurgling stomach, full of the goodness of the never-failing breast. Alone you were. In a closed world where your eyes could not focus beyond the edge of a pink frilled quilt, nor your ears define the melody of a tune hummed over cornflakes and scrambled eggs. She doing things but not with you. A jungle of imprecision and no words.

You are alone, as you were when you sucked at her teat, enclosed by her arms, as when you first walked from her knee to the chair in which you now sit. The solitude that you feel as you try to touch those that hurry past while trees grow, grass withers, corn ripens, apples fall, the wind blows. A river flows illuminated by the sun which sets to rise again and the tide ebbs. You are alone in the morning train, you are alone at the typewriter clattering desk, in the shop, while you order your lunch, swearing at the old slow man in front, in the bath and under the sheets at night snuggling close. You are alone. Silently weeping, talking, laughing, singing. You buy shoes, you dance.

You let the dentist meddle in your mouth and the doctor finger your pulse, your hair is cut but not by her and still you are alone.

You   Come, D, let us sit together.

The table is laid for dinner. A fine white cloth, candles, meat, wine, bread, a napkin by your plate. You're not sure which side, etiquette is not your strong point. Principles of protocol, glass in this hand, knife, fork, left handed. It's unimportant, shirts can be washed, the taste is unimpaired. Yes, your hand shakes, more as you grow older. You bend low over the plate, slurp a bit. You carry the cup and the saucer one in each hand to avoid the rattle. Life is not elegant. It includes messy places like school canteens and maternity wards with afterbirths and waters running out to spoil the cleanly polished lino. Everyone contributes to the sewage works.

You   So, your name is D?

D   No.

You   No? Ah, yes, correct. It begins with a 'd'.

Suddenly dying. Thoughts of the end, cemeteries, timid words, not to be spoken aloud but mumbled. Whispered through feelings, tears. The cold stone, carved, flowers plucked to beautify granite. Gold applied to gild the truth. All around stones poking up from the dead encasing ground. Widow's weeds sprout. Children don't look. This is where your father lies. Brambles, bushes, green leaves of elder. Traitor. Judas hanged himself on this pale twig. Took his life and denied the truth. Champagne flowers. Bees fertilise. Fruits fall. You brush past to read the inscription.

It is gone, faded, smooth. Illegible but for the faint shadows over the multigrey crystal surface like words which have sometime flown from your lips, unaware. An angel murmured and a keen ear heard. A name, a date, maybe a town. The dents from where the hammer fell have been eroded by the weather until only patience can read the briefest summaries of life histories. Born, named, died.

You face each other across the table. You smile dimly, hoping that your gesture will be returned. Your lips twitch. Somewhere, secluded in the tall bushes that surround the grave that is common to you both, lies a vestige of a love that once was not yet broken. The twitch is a promise of good times to come. Only today. Today contains the past and envisages the future but today is all there is. Would that this inner rage become calm, that this inability to express the grand desires be vanquished.

You   It is time to talk.

D   Certainly. Here I am.

You sit gazing out of the window and the trees grow while you sit, struggling to set words from thoughts.

Jesus was Jewish too. It's better out than in, the smell dissipates in the open. The smell from the death squads, with the rotting cabbage stalks and the cheese you never chewed. Ulcers. You have to declare that being a Jew is the same now as when Jesus was alive. You have to have the courage. Yes, if you like, you're a missionary but you don't propose to go screaming over the heads of the crowd because people can't hear like that. It comes from experience, yours. You must wait for theirs which is different. It will take time. You are not a genius. You're not going to set the world on fire. Trust the world. Auschwitz was terrible; and yet it will happen again.

You   So, declare yourself, a single initial is not much
             to go on. It must stand for something, an
             acronym, there must be more to you than one
             letter.

Words falling like blood, fine red droplets gathering speed. You have opened the wound and cannot staunch the flow. Beneath the tough skin you glimpse a vision of the truth.

There was a time when you viewed him as a giant which towered as a mountain face, unapproachable. You stood in the grass of the valley where hayricks were stooked to dry in the sun and you shouted. You hesitated. There was an echo. Indistinct. Perhaps the message that you yelled was rude, unintelligible, words from a child concerned with matters which he, the grown up, had long forgotten.

You played, not worried whether the reply was accurate, reflected truly. You called him names, He made puns and gave you questions to which the only answer was a joke. You never heard that you gave only those answers which he had already set in the words of the question. His pleasure was paramount. Then puns began to pall. You wanted truth but you had never learned how to ask so that he would speak of himself. Your phraseology was still uncouth. You argued, unwilling to listen. Thoughts became entangled with themselves, words were bunged up. His dreadful disapproval turned nouns and verbs into illness and disease. Worthiness became sham, the stillness of your room was shattered. You opened your lips to pose the question that you dearly wished to ask and from deep inside the scream vomited. Vile taste of murderous rage. The scream slammed from papered walls to cloth-covered table. It was the memory of the past. In the green fields where you stood you watched a shadow chasing your youth.

You begin to hear.

Do you see? The tall sycamore trees at the top of the bank are shining in the sunlight. Between the trunks a fox runs believing himself unseen. There are piles of old leaves turned over by birds. A patch of bluebells is running to seed.

What an initial letter can conjure. Across the table with his knees hidden by the white cloth, you sit, one on each side, facing.

You remember now, it was to please her that you would mop toothpaste from the bathroom shelf, that you would scrape the burnt bits off the toast, put your dirty clothes in the proper basket, take another piece when you weren't hungry, be polite when you felt offended, keep your temper when you didn't want it.

You   For you, D. An alphabet of names.

The difficulty is precisely this. To avoid him you are forced to provoke him. It's the ordinariness of living. You thump your way through the fat and the gristle, the knife falls, your front splatters with gravy. You pass from one mess to the next. Or you pretend. Fine dining. Waiters to remove the debris. New plates and clean knives. Men in grey coats approach the house by the door at the back. The bin is empty.

You will be frank. He wants the gold, the money, the power. He wants the control to say what should happen and when and where. Everything should go wrong so that it may conveniently be your fault. You have no idea why his name commences with a 'd'. Obdurate, indolent, idle, the 'd' is there but not beginning, all adjectives which he applies to you, damning you with epithets. You can never win the prize of liberty, the grand cry, brotherhood and equality to echo the chains which clank behind where you cannot see. Ultrastrong apron strings of carbon steel, twisted for tenacity, resistant to the sharpest knives, hooked for permanence. In the tentacles of her love you rest entwined. He need not worry that you may wander far, she has cleverly ensured that from the warmth of her womb you will desire no adventure. Suffocating, you will want to suffer more. You have learned to prefer smog to the cold wind of independence.

You are closer now. He has preyed on you for many days, loaded your body with guilt. You begin to hear.

He has peopled a multitude of critics sitting in the stalls, applauding, while you stumble around the stage. Bright lights illuminate your beads of sweat. You learn the lines, sing the songs and dance the tango on occasion. You act a fool to make him laugh, play a wise man for the tragedy. You smoke cigars for realism, bring pretend tears to your eyes, slap sticks with shaving cream, kiss girls, make love, and make your final exit. He applauds the wrong man. He is not you. You are the one who keeps silent, who dares not move. You wear your mask of paint, a disguise for reality. She, the divine darling of the producer, claps hands with a glass of cheap red wine. Her loud voice proclaims you in your role. You slouch in her lap, loll over her cigarette holder, admire her tortoise shell lunettes. She is your idol.

Your nerves are shattered, you will probably catch cold.

D   Did you say that you didn't believe in me?

You   Yes.

D   So why are you talking to me? Isn't that in conflict? You can't talk to someone if you don't believe they exist.

You pause, reflect.

You   So, I exist whether you believe in me or not.

D   Yes?

You   And you have the same right, to exist independently of whether I believe in you or not.

D   Yes.

Silence. You ask a question.

You   Why am I talking to you?

D   I don't know. Maybe you think I have something that you want.

You   Oh yes, that's for certain.

D   So, what do you want?

You   I don't know.

D   Oh.

You are silent, struck dumb.

Ah yes, now you see. He wants you to tell him what you want. How convenient, it absolves him from taking responsibility, a brilliant ploy.

D   But it won't work.

You   Why not?

D   Because I haven't a clue what you want.

You are alone.

Chapter 2
THE STATUE

Trafalgar Square in the City, a café
You, Dick, Nelson, a Waitress

From the position of the eyes the view is stupendous. You could see easily over the tops of even tall buildings to a stretch of parkland in one direction or to the ever-rising city blocks in the other. You could, that is you, because your eyes are movable in sockets, in a head that may be turned through several degrees on a neck that is reasonably flexible though stiffening with age. You would enhance the capacity to admire the view by rotating your shoulders and to some extent your hips but you would not be able to move your feet to turn a full circle since you would be obliged to hold on to your perch in order to maintain balance. Thus, there would be a part of the view that would remain hidden. However, it is not your eyes which are at this moment in the position from which the magnificent view is to be seen. Your eyes are somewhat lower down.

The correctly placed eyes are made of stone. They are wide open, unable to look anything other than slightly upwards in a direct gaze without the slightest deviation to left or right. You have not actually seen these eyes so you know nothing of the large tear drops which have collected in the lower lids ossifying over lengthy periods to a kind of nodule of hard flint. Neither are you aware that the eyes blink, the upper lids not quite closing the gap due to the accretions of the tears, even though the eyeballs themselves do not move. They remain fixed.

You have been requested to make a detailed observation of the fluted column which supports the statue. The column cannot actually be seen from where you are standing; it is obscured by an overhanging plinth. You step a few feet back and the whole column stretches above you. You notice how the lines of the fluting are broken at intervals where joints occur between the blocks of stone; you wonder how you will identify successive joints. You begin to appreciate the fineness of the curve but you have completely forgotten the name for this curve though you know it was invented by a famous Greek whose name you have also forgotten. These thoughts you communicate to Dick. You are certain that Dick will be impressed by the breadth of your knowledge. Dick thinks you are a prick. He knows this is true because you never go to the pub on Friday nights, you don't watch television, and you say that you were faithful to your wife. Dick also knows that you continually spout words in which he is not the slightest bit interested. His purpose in life is simple. He has told you many times that all he wants is enough money to live a life of luxury and ease. He talks to you at length about the latest objects of his desire and is at a loss to understand why you respond with such little enthusiasm. He has therefore concluded with full justification and ample evidence that you are a prick. He has even told you directly, but you are incapable of accepting this fact. You have accepted Dick as one of the young men with whom you work. You do not call him a yob although that is what he is; you are terrified of his driving habits; you are envious of his leather jacket, his wolf-whistle, his capacity to drink, his girlfriend, his wages, his new car and his smutty newspapers which you read surreptitiously; you are responsible for his education.

No-one has asked you to teach him, he is indifferent to your concern. Nevertheless, you teach him. Morals, ethics, the evils of drink, the wonders of language, art, science are all within your sphere. The more you talk the more Dick becomes aware of your ignorance and the more addicted he becomes to your company.

Dick is also in the business of education, but his method is more subtle. He knows that you will follow him because you are a prick. So far, he has shown you how to smash lightbulbs, deface posters, open car doors without a key, maintain full control while drunk. He has beguiled you with his stories of riches - his bird's father earns more in a month than you will in ten years - he knows that your car cannot match his for speed, he has seen through your facade of propriety and cleanliness. In short, he has twisted you around the end of his little finger.

Dick   What are we doing this for?

He has flipped the machine into action.

You have been requested to investigate the possibility of safeguarding the statue following a tremor which is believed to have cracked the pedestal. Your actual task is to determine the extent to which the pedestal is now out of plumb which, for you, will be a simple job of establishing a baseline, making a number of observations and calculating the answer. You are prepared to check your answer by using a secondary baseline which you will place near enough at right angles to the first and...

A wrapper from a bar of chocolate touches your trousers.

You are engrossed in the Latin inscription which is written continuously around the square base of the column. You recognise some names from your history books. You are astonished; you didn't know so many battles had been fought by this one man, but your Latin is not quite sufficient for you to understand the difference between battles fought and those alluded to. You point out to Dick the marvels of past ages. You describe in tedious detail how you had to miss out on history lessons and your head swells as you imagine with pride that you can remember the Latin you learnt. You make a vainly inaccurate translation of the inscription.

Dick wipes the chocolate from his lips. He is listening to you but not to your story. He is considering why you should pay so much attention to a statue and so little to the beautiful pieces who are crossing the square well within view. He is listening to you but not watching you. The women are neither listening to you nor watching Dick, but they are well aware of the potential energy which they have aroused.

Dick   Now, that is a beautiful piece of work.

You are in raptures. You glance upwards to admire the figure whose exploits you have so magnificently rendered but all you see is the plinth.

You   Dick!

Dick   What?

You continue the translation.

You are bored. Dick is bored. But you are going to persevere. Why don't you start work? Why do you play this farce of adoration of the statue? Who does he represent for you that you have to march around his base declaring to anyone who will listen, which doesn't include Dick, his feats and great achievements? You hear the questions and delay the answers. You know who, you know why. You know that you should be working. It is easier to play this game. It is the status quo. Nothing shall be done until you can be guaranteed that you will receive full and unlimited approval for any action which you might take, such approval being the means whereby you stay alive, without which you die, suffer starvation, loss of security. All is at stake.

You are back where you started.

Nelson   Could I tell you the true story?

You   By all means.

Nelson   I am here.

You   Yes, I can see you are.

Nelson   How? You have never been this high, not since I was installed. Nobody comes up to my platform.

You   Birds?

Nelson   They don't count. They sit, shit, flit, flap, scrap and squawk. I endure birds.

You   Sorry.

Nelson   No need. I require no pity. I am at ease. My coat is buttoned, my hat is fastened, the rain falls, I am washed, the sun has a negligible effect on the stone. I have been frozen, baked, shot at, illuminated, and regarded.

You   You must have seen great changes?

Nelson   None.

You   I beg your pardon.

Nelson   Don't.

You   I'm sorry.

Nelson   You always are.

You are looking up, can see but unclearly. You will have ample opportunity as soon as you have set up the tripod. Which, however, you are reluctant to do.

Nelson   The replacement of one edifice with another, the growth of brick and concrete in place of trees and grass, these are not great changes. Rather they are the pale manifestations of our inability to remain content with the way we found the world. I was the same. Nothing is new. I used to be able to see quite a long way across the river to the hills. The hills are still there. So are the seeds, the acorns, the beechmast and the pine kernels. But because you now see buildings, offices and blocks of flats, you imagine that the earth has changed, that life is somehow different. It is not so.

Look over there, beyond the hoardings, between the grey exposed faces of the buildings. Do you see a bomb site, ruins, great heaps of rubble? Or do you see where the rabbits have been, the buddleia growing, the old pram turned into an adventure playground?

You turn around slowly, caught in the middle of a dream. Dick has moved to the other side of the plinth. A bell rings at the edge of the square. It has a tune but the noise of traffic makes it impossible to hear anything more than faint reverberations.

Nelson   I was born in a hovel; I died in a palace.

My mistress…

There is a long pause.

You remember a phrase but cannot recall the details. There was some information, a kind of warning, precautions that you need to take, a form of assurance that what you were about to embark on was not an affair that would be over before the dawn. Somebody is telling you that you should always remember the consequences of your actions, that it is possible, honourable even, certainly not something to be dismissed lightly as a schoolboy joke, to take protective action. You were not listening then; you are listening now but the words have drifted. You knew all about that, it was common knowledge, everybody knew. But now it is different. Now it has connotations of shame, of missed opportunities, of not being able to further the seed. You sigh.

Nelson   At the age of seventeen I was sent to sea. It was a terrible ship. We ate biscuit.

After one year I had become captain. Let me tell you that there is only one way. Crow's nests, biscuit, the stink of powder, put up with them if you will. I did not and I saw to it that I rose rapidly until I could dictate what I should eat, where I should sleep and where I should sail.

And I am stuck here for one foolish mistake. I took on the French. Had I listened to my own advice which I had faithfully followed for months I would now be resting peacefully in a decent grave. But no, I was misled, not by my superiors, they are not to be blamed, but my own loss of self-awareness. One slip and I found myself embroiled in a broadside assault. I won, of course. That was the easy part. Anybody can win a battle. But I lost my freedom.

She wanted to marry me. I was the hero of the hour, they fêted me, carried me on their shoulders, it was a rough ride, but they meant well. I didn't fall off, there have been worse moments at sea, I was always sick. But I could do nothing against her.

Don't get me wrong, I loved her, passionately. I enjoyed the steamy nights under the covers. Bold explorations of her delights, her hands holding me, gave me such pleasure, finding the ways that our bodies could fit.

Night after night we discovered the glory of nature. We held each other as if the world would never end. The smoothness of her skin, the delicious taste, her scent, the glow of warmth when we had done. We lay for hours. I felt so wonderful during the day, I could do anything, I had energy, enthusiasm, boundless creativity. And now look at me, a poor stone creature.

You see this lacework of mess from the pigeons? It reminds me daily of the snare. I was enticed as if into a net. She drew me in, there was no effort, it was as natural to her as breathing. But it was the end. I fell into a lethargy of house husbanding.

You   I thought you were an admiral?

Nelson   Oh yes, I was a man of state. Banquets, affairs.

You   You mean with other women?

Nelson   Never!

You   You're very categoric on that score.

Nelson   Certainly and I have a right to be. It's true.

You laugh. Dick turns sharply but you don't see him.

You   I don't understand you. You complain to me that you have lost your freedom because you were forced into marriage.

Nelson   Oh no, I was not forced; I wanted to. That's the damnable thing about it. I was all ready to live with her, give her everything, till death us do part. No, it was the lack of awareness. I never stopped to think, perhaps one doesn't in those circumstances, it all seems so natural. You love her, you go to bed with her, you find that you have something in common, she's a decent girl, pretty, you have money, you get married. Simple. Grand wedding. Presents. Occasion. Honeymoon. Guests retired gracefully; we retired excitedly. Spectacular night, utter exhaustion, exhilaration for ever after.

You   So what went wrong?

Nelson   I told you. My freedom was gone, bang out the window.

You   This is boring.

Nelson   I know, nobody likes listening to a sob story. You carry on. Don't mind me. I'll still be here when you've done.

You are staring into the sky. Your eyes watch the head of the statue, mesmerised. Dick is at your side.

Dick   Come on, mate.

You   Yes.

One of those extra tea breaks. Taken in a cafe where the walls were once finely decorated but the stain of tea has browned everything to a shade of light tan. The tables are too narrow for everyone to put their elbows on. There is a newspaper on the chair, an ashtray, men sit in dull conversation. A young man plays a fruit machine, not because he expects to win but because his friends expect him to play. He plays. He wins. He plays. The money goes in, the wheels spin, the lights flash and the money runs out. He loses.

Dick drinks his tea.

Waitress   Yours love?

She has a broken homely look. Too much frying.

Dick   Bloody machine.

Waitress   Egg and chips?

He scoffs, dousing the taste with ketchup and salt.

While you. Gaze at the tea which you would stir if you had the nerve to put sugar in it, but your sense of morality is too strong. Fatness will inherit the grave and so will you, but you will die virtuous.

Nelson   I told you.

You are startled, you have been seen. From behind the tall houses the statue is visible, the carved cockatoo topped hat peeks from over the roof tops.

Waitress   You all right, darling?

This is complicated, first him, then her.

You   Yes, love, I mean, oh.

You feel the beads of perspiration. You didn't mean to call her love, but her attitude is one of mothering all who come into her eating house. She hovers near your chair, her breasts beneath the plastic apron pointing visibly at you. She enquires into your requirements. She has behind her an array of comforters in the shape of sausages with bubble and squeak, soft rolls filled with grated cheese, puddings of sponge with syrup sauce.

You   No, I'm not really hungry.

Nelson   You see, this is precisely what I mean. You are lost forever once you enter the arms of the female.

A flock of pigeons punctuates the air. Dick slurps his tea leaving smears of yellow yolk. You pay the bill. She looks at you and you, not wishing to appear disrespectful to the proprietress of a cafe, return her look.

Dick   Liar.

The jumble of voices rises to a babble of commands, instructions, orders to be obeyed.

Waitress   Thank you, love.

Dick   You're far too serious.

Waitress   Here's your change, mind now, how you go.

Dick   You ought to do it yourself sometimes, you know, it's a real education.

            Listen to me, it is the truth that I am telling you.

Nelson   Real life, he means.

You push at the swinging door, loaded with tripods, guilt and feelings. Her bosom would welcome you; the stony gaze dares you not, your own admonitions hesitate and the challenge from Dick is better ignored. Your hands reach the safety of your pockets where they remain tightly fisted clutching at loose cotton and a shrivelled paper tissue.

The air outside is cooler and the nape of your neck is sweaty through the tension of the strap which carries the weight of the tripod; reason makes a fool of anyone. Inside you are mixed, tea is a bitter herb, your stomach is not gratified by your unwillingness to feed yourself with bacon or eggs or chips or any of the other richly deserving foods of the poor unwhetted child within. You are sullen, accusing Dick of perversity. Sexual matters are clearly on your mind and you have decided to deny them; you favour finding fault.

You   Bollards!

            Why don't they make the traffic one way?

27

Dick has his own preoccupations, healthier, more diverting.

Dick   Now she needs me!

You kick at a penny on the pavement. Never waste anything. Mottos and morality.

Dick   Aren't you going to pick it up? I've seen you before, doing it, rubbing off the dirt, slipping it slyly into your pocket.

Cockatoo spies all. Through buildings, hoardings, trees, hills, parklands, beaches, his sight through hardened teardrops can be bent to any direction. The all-seeing guardian of an elderly gentleman perched at a vantage with pigeons for fellows and steeplejacks for visitors, his sculptor's name emblazoned on his shoes, he watches all your moves. You may have determined by observation that his gaze is directed towards a particular and invariable point in the middle horizon as viewed from his standpoint but your logic, while valid in the school-room, cannot be bent whereas his line of sight is as flexible as the mind of God.

Who was it who taught you this? You cannot hide from your conscience.

Chapter 3
SUITCASE
In the square
A Suitcase, Nelson

The suitcase is innocent. It is made of not guilty cardboard covered in guilty, because not real, pretend leather made to look like smell impregnated, pores imprinted, but honestly not, so probably extremely guilty plastic, born in a factory, conceived in a managing director's head, clothed with clasps and hinges, ornamented with initials, scratches and tags.

The clasps are of brass look, of cheap pressed steel with padlocks of millimetric dimensions and pretentious keys, two, suitable as weights for an airmail feather but not for locking suitcases. The hinges considered of no importance, extruded from hot moulds, pinned with bright metal rods and left, unfinished. The initials wrong, gilt, faded, daft. The tags old, outmoded, snobbish, indicating holidays desired but not taken, romances embarked on, realities discounted, lovers met and never seen again, dark nights, bright days. The scratches real.

The clasps keep the innocent space inside the already death-sentenced cardboard closed from the dubious influences of the heavy city air. The hinges do the backside bottom base of their suitcase job. Their job they do with no complaints allowing the lid to be opened, shut, squeezed, closed at the owner's whim, by baggage handler, luggage thief, porter, inquisitive wifely eye, and customs officer.

Shut.

Inside is murky smell. It is dark. No hint of light from the dent in the side. The weight of the contents, plastic wrappings, sandwich papers, used up biros, comb, book, bookmark, page 92, have I read this bit, maybe, maybe, time sheets filled in, box, old watch, nail file, plasters just in case, matches, egg shell, how did that get in there, old picnic, memories of brown bread, yellow yolk, yoke of old, youth no more, mis-spent money, youth gone, and it went, taken from, given out, gone, gone, gone.

Suitcase   Ha! Innocent. Not my fault. Yes, I did it, but I didn't know.

Nelson   Ignoramus. Weightlifter.

Case to be filled, portable, carried, dumped in racks on buses, trains, in the boots of cars, snoozing in the dark, trundled on carousels, inspected, chalked on, labelled, called for, weighed but not found wanted. The suitcase was innocent. It meant no harm to anyone. It was the filler, the lifter, the carrier. Him. Unaware of its position in the world, swinging there at the end of his arm, burdened with his belongings, the ones he wanted with him.

Knocked.

Suitcase   It was an accident, you understand.

The suitcase going backwards and forwards in the nether space between waist and heel where no-one ever looks. Knocks into the tripod, bounces a bit, carried relentlessly by the hand that holds its handle. Looks back.

Suitcase   Sorry mate, can't stop, being hurried. Carried. Job to do.

But the tripod doesn't bounce. Long thin telescopic legs not the bouncy sort. Three don't bounce. Three legs resting on tips on the foot smooth paving. Slabs of York stone hewn from quarries, not in York, where, when, don't know, don't care. The tripod was placed with the utmost intention, levelled, plumblined, directly centred over the nail which marked the spot.

Dick had hammered the nail. He had been careful. Dick is now beginning to run. He had been told to use that nail. Erect the tripod. Run. Curse and run, you fucking suitcase. Can't you see?

Legs of telescopic tripod splay. Tripod mounted cut glass prism. Held erect. Valuable, hundreds.

Suitcase pulls back, bounces to its owner's hand.

Tripod becomes bipod becomes unipod. Unipod on one leg has no balance, topples over. Prism looks upwards to the sky instead of straight ahead like the stony statue's gaze. Dick's face horror struck. Suitcase now mingling in legs of crowd. Prism now turning away from sky, past direct gaze of stony statue, past faceless facades of stony buildings that march in silence round the square.

Crash.

Suitcase is gone.

Prism is upside down. Multi-faceted face on the cold slabs where feet tread and dogs do. Cut precisely to reflect the image light back from where it comes. Silvered for the finest image. Light ray, enter in, light ray, reflex out, in, out, same light. Upside downside left right polarised silver tainted cracked not whole ray light still will work again.

The prism is unbroken. The tripod has three legs.

Dick sets the prism over the nail.

A slight difference in the height of the tripod in its newly erected stance. A variation in the angle of the head of the prism. Slight, a nuance.

Cockatoo takes note.

Chapter 4
COCKATOO
The Zoo

You, a Matron, a Young Woman, Inspector Daks

The origin of Cockatoo is a trip to the zoo where the particular plumed figure is noticed standing on a perch. There are bars between you and it is a matter of debate according to one's point of view as to which is the safe side. You suppose that your side is secure because you believe your parents and especially your uncle. However, Cockatoo, for his part, suffers under an equal delusion that he is safe on his side of the bars. The actual purpose of the bars has nothing to do with security; they are a relic of attempts to remain out of reach of excitement.

Cockatoo sidles over.

Your eye, brown, and his, yellow, compare notes; his of the relative frequency of blinking, yours of the relative sizes. Your mind, blank, and his, vacant, do not bother to think.

Cockatoo speaks.

To the extent that none of the words he uses will be found in the dictionary his speech is unintelligible, but the tone is unmistakably one of derision and mockery. You assume that he has spoken for your benefit alone, you pretend to follow the message delivered and you fancy that you could retort in a way that you would like to learn Cockatoo's language.

He replies by pecking at your thumb which you have inadvertently curled around the bar of the cage.

You withdraw rapidly but continue your interest in what the bird has to say, chiding him, moving ever closer to his territory. He pecks again but bites metal.

Cockatoo   Ouch!

You   Clever, aren't you?

With both a desire to provoke the bird and the possibility of making friends you remove from a plastic carrier bag a half-eaten Chelsea bun which you present directly to Cockatoo's face. Whereupon, Cockatoo stiffens, half raises his wings, opens his beak to protest and falls stone dead to the floor.

There is a murmur amongst the visitors and a matronly looking elder woman, clad in a gorgeous fur coat, rises above them. She pulls you away from the bars by your sleeve.

Matron   That is an offensive weapon.

You   Which, the bun or the carrier bag?

Matron   Fool.

You   Madame, you could be right.

To show willing you tell her you will eat the rest of the bun and you will demonstrate the safety of the bag.

You   Would you guard this for me?

You hand a younger woman, clad in blue serge, the bun and cover your head with the bag, searching for one of the small air holes which you know are always there but after a few moments you are forced to pull the bag off, gasping for breath.

Most of the spectators decide that there is no more interest in the scene. However, the young woman to whom you have handed the bun is looking at it carefully. She is scratching at it with her filed fingernail, but it is obviously extremely hard, quite inedible, and whilst the currants are clearly visible and the texture of the bun still has the appearance of a crumbly consistency there would seem to have been a metamorphosis since its baking, purchase and semi-consumption. She scrapes the outside on which the sugar crystals glisten expecting some of them to be dislodged but they are permanently consolidated into the baked surface. She taps the broken surface where it is indented around the edges by your teeth marks. She lifts the bun to her ear and taps again. It is a strange object.

Woman   How old is this bun?

Matron   The age is of no consequence, the question is its capacity to be used as a lethal weapon.

Woman   Madame, I was not asking you.

You protest that it is a perfectly ordinary Chelsea bun which you bought only this morning in a perfectly ordinary bakery. There are dozens of them in London as there are several other specimens of this parrot family in the country.

Matron   Would you pass me the bun, please?

Woman   Madame.

Matron   Perfect and ordinary are contradictory in terms. It is either perfect in which case it is unlikely to produce a bun which becomes so inedible after such a short time or it is ordinary in which case the bun could not possibly have been employed as a weapon but there may be alternative explanations.

A man barges in.

Man   Show us your hat with feathers.

Matron   I beg your pardon?

Man	Why do you go around pretending to be something you aren't? You wear the skin of a fox or rather several foxes and underneath you hide your hat made up of white feathers, all from cockatoos.
Matron	Preposterous.
Man	Exactly so, especially when you are accusing this man of killing the same bird which is now sitting once again on its perch.

The situation is becoming confusing and calling for explanation. However, events are moving too rapidly for you to analyse fully the symbolic significance of all the characters and you resort to violence. You seize the edge of the matron's fur coat to expose the hat of white feathers.

The lady is naked. She screams.

Cockatoo slumps and the man who has made the accusation about her hat removes his own coat to reveal that he is in uniform. He proceeds to question you and her asking both of you simultaneously.

Man	Why have you got nothing on? Why have you eaten the evidence? And why have you lost your mind?
You	I.
Matron	He.
Woman	She.

The young woman retrieves the bun.

Woman	This is the weapon, Inspector. It is a piece of stone cunningly painted to look like a bun.
You	No, it is a bun, I've only just bought it.
Woman	Then tell me why it's so hard?
You	Who are you?

She has an undeniably beautiful face. Dressed in the blue serge overalls which enhance her femininity they suggest a supple and lithe figure which they clothe. Despite her interrogation you smile at her and then almost immediately begin to blush unable to hide your embarrassment at being challenged by her nubile person. Her overalls are not as dark nor as smart nor with such fine buttons nor with any braid at the epaulettes as the man who is now facing you with a very fine straight moustache and penetrating eyes.

Daks   I am Inspector Daks of the Metropolitan Force.

You   So, what difference does that make?

His arm is restrained by the presence of the naked lady who is putting her coat of fur back on allowing you to turn away from his questions to the attractive woman in the blue serge uniform.

Woman   This so-called bun, rock-cake, is solid granite and has been exquisitely carved and ornamented to make it appear like an edible object.

She hands it to the Inspector. As you stare at the pink flesh holding the yellow pastry a moment of fear enters your vision. The bun slips through the fingers of Inspector Daks' outstretched hand and shatters.

Everyone, except you, bends down to pick up the pieces. Why do you not join them? Why do you stand rooted to the spot, unable to flinch even a muscle? Are you about to join Cockatoo in his descent from the perch? Have you perceived what Cockatoo had seen when first presented with the imitation Chelsea bun? Have you seen in the shards the medusine nature of the cake of stone? You awake but in a trance to hear Cockatoo whisper from the floor of the cage. In front of your eyes swarm the serpents that clothe the head of the Gorgon.

Do you know where you came upon the terrible weapon? Do you know in what dreams you have managed to steal upon the hideous monster and sever her head? Do you know by which alchemy you have converted its form into the half-eaten Chelsea bun?

Cockatoo closes his eyes.

Daks   Now, Sir, we have here a serious crime and I shall require you to accompany me to the guard-house.

You   Officer, I can't move.

Daks   Nonsense. Put one foot in front of the other. Let me assist you by attaching your hands to these attractive bracelets.

You   For a Cockatoo that isn't even dead? Come off it. And besides, I tell you I can't move.

Inspector Daks looks at the cage where the cockatoo lies motionless on the hard concrete floor, his beak partly open in an attitude of shock and his wings stiffly jutting into the air. The Inspector jiggles up and down the remaining crumbs of the Chelsea bun, listening to the metallic sounds in his palm.

Daks   It's as dead as a dodo.

You look at the bird yourself and with an ordinary glance its demeanour would not have led anyone to think that it had any life within it but you are quite certain that you have heard it speaking.

Daks   Stop acting!

You   An act? No, I'm telling you I can't move.

Blue serge and fox skins begin to dance with the gleaming buttons on the uniform of Inspector Daks whose moustache turns slightly upwards to hold hands with the curved crest of Cockatoo. It is a masquerade through the crowd of people who have come as visitors to the zoo, gathered to watch animals doze in dark corners, to glimpse them on the edges of pools and rocks, to guess at sleeping forms in cages and thorny enclosures where timber poles hold out dead branches in memory of trees, where ornate letterings announce the presence of lions and monkeys and the jungle consists of a diverse humanity alienated by walls, moats and iron railings. It is Babel come to the zoo. Everyone foreign to everyone else, each exploring the already found, each speaking as though the other understands. It is as meaningful as the grunt of the llama.

A penguin slips into the water of a blue tiled Antarctic paddling pond and an eagle stretches its wings to see whether the bars of its cage have moved any further apart. A gorilla vomits and eats its own sick.

You   What was that?

You are musing that all these poor creatures have to have something to do to maintain the pretence.

Daks   The pretence?

Daks knows that scientific research is the primary aim of the zoological gardens. He admits that the public might be amused; they should be allowed to pay for the pleasure of allowing the staff to continue with their proper work. Something like that anyway. Not in the brochure but probably in the terms of reference, the job description. All these birds and things.

You   What are you talking about?

Daks   This bird thing, this cockatoo, is here under false pretences, imprisoned for no crime but to gratify a motive passed to us by generations of cataloguers. His purpose is to stay alive as best he can within the circumstances.

You   You mean cage.

Daks   Precisely.

Cockatoo winks.

You   You see?

Daks   Wait a moment, do you work in this place?

You   No.

Daks   Who are you exactly?

You   Exactly? I don't know myself. But approximately, as near as you can get to the truth, although not enough to satisfy you, my friend, Inspector Daks, I am a sculptor, a prison visitor, land surveyor. I live alone in an apartment which I have decorated with pictures and where I bake fresh bread, my parents are both dead and my lover has disappeared. More than that I would like to know myself.

Inspector Daks muses. On which side of the bars are you a visitor to the prison? He who bakes bread may also make Chelsea buns. Do sculptors carve stone to imitate life? Is blue serge another disguise for nakedness? Is your lover now vanished not also present at the scene of the crime?

Daks   Young lady, you will also join the party in the guard house.

Cockatoo lies dead still.

Woman   Party?

Daks   Enough. These stones.

He picks out one of the larger pieces and gives it to her. She eats it.

Woman   Not bad. Quite soft, actually. Nice currants.

Inspector Daks assumes an air of unshockability, hesitates, feels the hardness, sniffs and eventually tries a bit.

Daks   It's stone!

The belief in the propositions of logical cause and effect have taken a strong hold in the mind of Inspector Daks whose feelings are of no account. If you know what you ought to do you should do that, you are obliged, knowledge and order, establishment of the cause and rectification of the fault. The future is a natural and fully explainable extension of the past. In the end the great harvest of what you sowed yesterday will be yours to reap tomorrow. It is all simple as long as you take the trouble to work it out. His face is a storm of wrath.

Daks   Where did you buy this thing?

You   In a shop.

Daks   Where?

You   It's not there anymore.

Daks   Where was it, for Christ's sake?

Could you repair this loss of memory so that the meticulous recorder could satisfy himself with your words in his notebook? You may have been scared to let it happen; what is relevant to you is the flow of time from present to present which an act of writing can freeze. Time is your comrade with whom you move like an orchestra in full voice resounding with anger and exultation, a gloomy silence and a pensive lull. And, though the notes and events might be sifted, weighed and analysed and William Daks might wish to classify them, you belong to the undivided universe.

You   I can't remember.

Daks   But you said you only just bought it.

Only and just are relative terms. How do you explain the circumstances in which the bun came to be yours? The slow forces of erosion visibly alter the world while an explosion may consist of infinite happenings each lasting a lifetime.

You   Yes, it was in a cakeshop.

Who had given you the instructions, the directions? The purchase of the bun? You had paid more than you had. Then, as you watch under the glittering pupils of Inspector Daks' eyes which examine your glazing over eyes, the street recedes into the past. It is not there anymore, it had been there when you needed it, the shop, the cake-lady, the penny pieces in your palm. Hardened with age.

You smell the breath of Inspector Daks and feel his strong hand gripping your wrist.

Daks   You're under arrest.

Cockatoo whistles.

Chapter 5
QUESTION TIME

A Guardroom

You, Inspector Daks, the Young Woman

To the Inspector of the Metropolitan Police the answer is not yet clear but he is certain that he can unravel the confusion. He is a man of truth, which is simple and to be found in books. A man who believes that salvation derives from following in the footsteps of his master. The pure life is free from sin and though temptations abound for the unwary, for the man of grace they may be easily hurdled.

You look around the walls. Speech coming at you from within and without. Yellow is the predominant colour though sunlight is not yet visible.

You notice the similarity between characters. Of course. Not stupid. D. Daks. All the same really. One in the past, one in the present, all conspiring for the future.

Future? A time within walls. A place without walls. A city to be built. Time to be. You could ask him for an extension. Use a longer sentence. Take your time to explain the origin of the bun, the bird. The bird still lying. Telling half-truths. Like D. Pulled up short as you went about your lawful business. In the zoo. At least there was space between the bars, between the cages, the fanciful houses for half related species, and unrelated stories. Caught up by fascination. Words half remembered, feelings half felt. Blood in the air. Fine red droplets gathering speed. Streaking past the predominant yellow of the walls, silent against the hum of machinations in the inspector's breast. Clean up. Take a break. Enjoy the present.

Daks   Sit down.

A cactus on top of the filing cabinet. Who waters it? Itself? Perhaps it is to beautify the room or perhaps the spines are symbolic of questions too sharp to answer.

Daks   This shop?

The prickles point in all directions.

You   Could have been anywhere.

Daks   But it was a particular shop.

It is a question. Spiny.

You   Must have been.

Daks   You mean there were alternatives?

On the other side of the cactus. Like the moon. It leaves you with a single choice. A pattern of ribs and vales each originating in the dry soil at the base, growing, broadening, giving room for collections of spines, before thinning to the crown. Does it ever flower? Under what conditions do blooms appear?

You   No, it was an actual baker's shop.

Daks   With a shopfront?

The cactus did flower. At some time in the past, yet to be elicited, it blossomed.

Daks   And a door?

From the roots, probing, searching out the dampness, sliding over grit, tasting nutrients. There is a way in by osmosis, without violence, into the body of the spine-protected plant. You entered by pushing at the sign marked 'Push'. The shop admitted you into its enclosing space.

Daks   Describe the window.

44

What colour was the flower, some gaudy flushing pink?

You   Glass.

Inspector Daks is distressed. To see through you without so much as a window blind into the depths of your murderous soul he is prevented. The reflection, instead, comes back at him and he dares not recognise the image. A grizzled stubby beard, unshaven for days. He washes his own body with total concentration in a daily ritual of privacy that removes him from the scenes of crime. His bathroom is scented, scrubbed and filled with steam. Good hot water and plentiful to wash away the sins of his blood. Razors, knives, toothpicks, brushes, stones of pumice, hard tough materials to soften the skin. A cold shower to finish off, keeps you healthy, father knows. Then warm towels remind him of his mother, dead now, God bless her soul. Ablutions are his second commandment, next to Godliness. If Satan tries to enter by his pores he will find no foothold of dirt, no cranny of evil. Satan is firmly flushed beyond the bend.

Daks   What did you see behind the glass?

What do you see in her blue serge, concealing flesh gaudy pink? The flower of her virginity. Surely not. And yet it is still possible. Why else should she be feeding animals, waiting for you, the prince who will release her from the spell of sexual torpitude. Did you dare to ask her? She held the bun. Are you also caught in the spell? She knew the trick of the cockatoo.

You   Why do you have a guardhouse in the zoo?

Daks   I ask the questions.

Perhaps the guardhouse satisfies an urge. To prevent the removal of blue serge. Perhaps the cactus has buds now, ready for the next blossoming. In any event, this will be a temporary residence.

Daks   What did you see behind the glass?

How do the buds form? What kind of stimulus provokes the initial urge? If it is passing of uniforms they would have to be of a particular kind. Uniform buds. Or is it some chance event in the wind, a warming of the air, like the glow of yeast in the shop? All producing diverse flowers. You didn't eat the whole bun and it may appear that you were easily satisfied but now with hindsight you see her lithe body passing close to your nose. It is a warm breath of air, a perfume that awakens your own body, sending pulsing blood to parts previously dormant and now hot for action.

You   A scent.

Daks   Aha! So you entered the shop.

And you recognise the perfume before the buds have burst, exposing their fragrant stamens. What smell mingles with your musky wanting, hoping she will wait for you, in her lonely room, preparing herself to meet you between darkness and light. A few hours here will intensify desire so that when you enter she will saturate your nostrils, drawing you closer, into a bond of passionate lovemaking.

You   No, it was a fantasy.

The cactus plant is fleshy, dull, green with not even the hint of a bud. The flesh is cuspy, a rhythm of long sharp spines at intervals all over its surface, expressing the acute chance of an explosion of anger should a foreign body attack.

How long do you stay in this position? Through a dull sensation of heat, you observe the floor tiles. The floor itself is cold so the heat must come from another source. The floor seems to be very close and it alternates between being in and out of focus. It is making a great deal of noise; its flatness echoes in your ears. For some reason you cannot move. Is this the Chelsea bun? Cockatoo? No. You have an impulse to raise yourself, unlike the previous occasion when all impulse was gone.

You   You hit me.

It is a statement. The cactus declares itself, the cockatoo, the fox skin lady, blue serge. Expressed out loud, not intended for comment or reply.

Daks   I'll hit you again.

You bounce.

Daks   I ask questions for one reason and for one reason only. I want answers, answers that make sense, logical sense. When I receive your answers I will write them down in my notebook and you will sign it as the truth, the logical rational truth. It will be a pride to you in the years to come, you will appreciate my help.

You consider the benefit of a defence of thorns. You rub your neck and look for the chair but your hand is lost in space. Perhaps your eyes are not fully open, perhaps in your fall you have become re-orientated, perhaps you could lie for a while on the floor.

Daks   Get up.

The lower drawer of the filing cabinet opens and you collapse over its rim. Your eyes are open now and you stare into its empty space. Paper clips.

The drawer is slammed shut. Does the cactus scream when its thorns are pulled out? Is the guardhouse soundproof? Nobody comes.

How long does the cactus wait from one watering to the next? If you press your finger tip into the dry soil. There will be no flowers on the cactus this year.

Daks	You bought the bun.
You	I bought the bun in a shop with a door and a window display and the door said push so I pushed and the door opened and when I went in there was a scent of yeast and rolls and loaves of bread on the shelves and cakes in the window and the woman in the shop was standing behind the counter and she said what did I want so I pointed at that one there and I bought a Chelsea bun.
Daks	You ate the bun.
You	I ate part of the bun, saving the uneaten part in its paper bag.

Can a cactus learn a catechism?

Daks	Aha!

The inspector screams.

Daks	Intention - murder! Motive - unknown. Method - concealed weapon!
You	No.

You hit the floor for a third time but this time your hand is holding onto the metal casing of the filing cabinet which judders slightly. Perhaps the floor will understand. But it does not.

Daks	Fool!

No, intelligence is not a factor. It's not a matter of logic or rational argument or anything like that.

His boot makes violent contact with the metal casing. And after the echo of the drums there is silence. A sharp heat enters your neck. How can you alleviate yourself of the pain of the policeman's questions? You ease the spines from your skin.

Daks	I ask questions because I want answers.

You grow old in the pause of his breath which smells of half-digested breakfast gulped down with lukewarm coffee. It could be the source of all troubles. Not enough food in the world. Always hungry. Angry for what you cannot get. Sucking harder but only ever hurting, never obtaining.

You   I have my rights.

Daks   Like hell!

Is it worth counting the number of spines? Perhaps it is only the feeling that remains, the pain is from the intrusion of the foreign body into yours. A single spine comes free between your fingers and you place it on the floor beside the split body, the shards of clay and the granules of earth. You observe the shortness of the roots. No, intelligence is not a factor. But then what is? How can you convince the interrogator of your innocence when you are not even sure yourself of what happened? Perhaps you do have powers of offence.

Inspector Daks is still. He is sifting the evidence in his mind, which except for one matter would be admirable. For in mind, Inspector Daks is certain of well-considered logic, starting with premise A, adding B, taking account of C and so forth until by deduction and some inspired guesswork the solution converges to a single conclusion. It is an inevitable process although occasionally, he admits, it takes time if one wishes to preserve neatness. He has the evidence, hard and soft, tasty, inedible, harmless, dangerous. But evidence, nonetheless.

Cockatoo smiles.

Daks   This bun.

Stony serpents.

You   A shop, a baker's, or a cake shop. Well, a shop.

And the cactus. It could have flowered, you know, given time and water.

Cockatoo frowns. The cactus unpotted and the shop no longer within reach, the need for their existence may have expired.

The real confusion is in time which we observe as passing along a unidirectional avenue; or in space which we conceive of as existing in an omnidirectional span. The carving of the statue and the disintegration of the same all come from apparently nowhere and everywhere and not one precedes the other nor has any extra value through having been and not now being. That is the trouble which Inspector Daks is having with the evidence.

Cockatoo ruffles his feathers.

Daks   It was edible when you had it first.

You   I tasted it.

There is no immunity in the past. Eventually all things turn sour and must be destroyed. Or disregarded.

Cockatoo laughs.

Only in the black mirror of your dreams may they be observed without harm. And in your dreams you will be given wings to your feet that will carry you wherever and whenever you wish to try. Your dreams are not limited to plodding like the badger across the surface of the world.

Listen to him. Inspector Daks is busy in his book. Writing. Suspect. You might imagine that he takes out a pipe which he fills with calm anticipation, pressing the fibres into the bowl, savouring the smoke. He does not. His shoulder droops slightly.

Just try to understand how something can, at the same time, be edible and potentially lethal. Difficult.

Impossible. No-one can reconcile such opponents. They are kept apart like day and night, east and west. He called you a fool and he was right. Your foolishness lies precisely in your attempt to converse with him when you do not speak the same language.

Daks   Get up.

You gaze at the broken cactus on the floor. A sudden thought enters your mind; are they poisonous? Will the questions continue to haunt you after your release from the blank walls of his mind? You rub the back of your neck. No more thorns. Then a second thought. Perhaps she is waiting for you. No buds, no flowers. How long can patience last?

Cockatoo snorts.

Awareness. If you have fancies, express them. What is made explicit no longer has the power to haunt us. Capture them. They are like ghosts until we use their spirit. But he has you in his command. You would believe all things and none of your own.

Beyond the zoo, beyond the fences that encircle these animals whose lives are proscribed by the same circumstances of fate as yours, beyond the feeding troughs, the yellow walls and the rich tea biscuits in the guardhouse, away from the hurly of the litter dropping public, another question is being asked. Maybe you can hear this question even though the person who asks it is silent.

Cockatoo turns his head to one side.

A man stares at the plate in front of him as it steams into the light from a bulb that hangs unadorned from the ceiling. The gravy on the plate thickens slightly and he feels a sense of revolt, of stuff being ingested, digested and eliminated. He is suffused with a mixture of sadness and anger, too strong to be dismissed, permeating him, leaving no space for food, sapping his energy.

His head collapses. A groan spills slowly onto the florets and embroidered leaves of the tablecloth so that the linen is washed in salt water. A storm unblocks the channels of neglect and the noise of his crying passes through the plaster and the blockwork to neighbouring rooms where other life continues. A family illuminated by the flickering blue light of a television screen hears the Gunfight at OK Corral. A typist lifts her hand momentarily from a keyboard. An old woman snoozes. Beyond the chimney flues the sound diminishes as it rises towards clouds and empty space. Only in the gardens below, among plants, a gardener hears the anguish of a man.

Every attempt has brought him closer to an edge. If he were to step over the edge, he imagines that there would be no more future. It would be like going outside his front door and finding nothing but the doormat beyond which there is no street, no horizon, no building on the other side. He has stared blankly into disbelief. He has tried praying that when he approaches this point in his life there might be a hint of something to look forward to. Instead, he sees a mist without shadows; a lack of surface on which to tread. The doormat is his last solid standpoint.

Now, he picks up the greasy plate and slides it into the washing up, swirls the water, rinses it and slots it into the rack where it will stay clean for another time. He selects his coat for the day and quietly pulls the door behind him.

The inspector slams down the remains of the bun on the table.

Daks   Look! Rock hard!

Blueserge	Yes, I know. I wondered about that too, and it was edible, I ate some, but I didn't like the taste.
Daks	Poison!
Blueserge	At a distance?

Cockatoo crows.

The doormat is inside. You say nothing. You are irritated. In discomfort. You bend down to replace the plant in its soil and simultaneously the inspector calls someone to clear up the mess so that while you are still engaged in pressing the dry earth around the cactus you catch a scent that you have smelled before this day.

You	Blue Serge!
Daks	So, you remember the name?
You	The name?
Daks	Of the baker.
You	She's not a baker, is she?
Blueserge	I may be. You are yourself.
You	Only an amateur.

So what are you waiting for? Godot? Permission?

Cockatoo is dismayed.

You had a good conversation going - it may have been a bit one-sided but to be fair you had only just begun.

| Blueserge | Here, Bill, catch! |

The badger barks, the bird shrieks and blue serge hurls herself into the noise of the crowd. Has the whole city come to ogle the animals. She gives no answer, at least not one you can hear in the tumult. You move swiftly across wrappings and droppings, turning between fences and patches of thorn, over lawns worn smooth by parties of children, reaching the turnstiles at the edges of the zoo. Behind you there is a crescendo as if the whole place was suddenly at feeding time, portions of vegetable and animal matter, some dead, some alive, being tossed in a crazy roller coaster of fodder. Don't throw up. Even Cockatoo is right now busy. Everything stops for the devouring of the innocent. Blood and saliva dribble from the jaws of the carnivores and the sight is no less pretty elsewhere. Bits drop to the side, hay gets trampled, skins fall to become slimy with age. A woman in a kiosk gleams with ecstasy. Her face is puffed, her sustenance is wrapped in rainbow colours and she sells it to the eye-popping faces who hold out pennies across the counter. The anticipation of satisfaction is too much: blue serge pushes you through the creaking stile.

Another time old friend.

Chapter 6
THE OLD LADY'S STORY

A street and then a sitting room upstairs
You, Blue Serge, an Old Lady, a Nurse

It is now your turn to be asking the questions. There are many facts you would like to know, her name, why she rescued you, where she lives, whether she is interested in sex, where you are going, how she knew, whether she works there full time, how old she is, what she has on underneath the blue serge, why you are going so fast, whether there might be a form of transport you could use, who she lives with, how comfortable her bed is.

Blueserge   We'll go down here.

You glance at the road sign, Belgrove Avenue. Meaningless. Not in your A-Z. A street lined with trees and cars and, beyond them, a terrace of houses. All doors, windows, some painted, avoiding bushes overhanging garden walls. She walks with purpose.

You   Could we slow down a bit?

Blueserge   Of course.

You   I mean, slow right down. There's nobody following and as far as I know they're all too busy at the moment.

She stops. You look at her with love in your heart. Observe her. Gentle smile, full lips, cheeks a pale rose, her eyes attract you. Messages begin to pass in the space between your faces. Her gaze is at you in the same way that your gaze is at her. The hunger for a companion may even be mutual.

Blueserge   What's your name?

You tell her.

You   Emil.

           Emil Finch.

Blueserge I like that, it has a rhythm to it.

You ask her.

Blueserge Melinda.

Your hand moves towards hers. You feel the harshness of her blue serge uniform and guess that inside there is a softer skin. You walk. Belgrove Avenue becomes Kendale Street which in its turn becomes another street and another. Names lose relevance.

You   Melinda, where are we?

The houses are tall blocks, the pavements are obstructed with long cars which were once expensive, there are broken bricks and remnants of sand. A dog slinks along the line of worn stone steps. There is little light between the rooves and the scent of elegance has been replaced by a smell of boiled cabbage.

Melinda   You don't live here, do you?

You   I've never been here in my life.

The street is long. You must have been walking for a long time, arm in arm, heeding neither traffic nor signposts. What you have discovered is feeling, a warmth made by the blending of spirits. You stop, hold each other around the waist and you notice that the light is fading. A chill wind makes you glance upwards at the houses where you see a face looking specifically at yours through the gap in the net curtains.

You're not sure how you came inside nor what happened to Melinda but here you are in a sitting room. There is a light which comes from a yellowing shade over a bottle shaped lamp which sits among papers, photos, and a box of Meltis fruit jellies on a dark mahogany table. The room is filled with mementos which mean everything to the old lady sitting in an armchair by the window and nothing to you.

Old lady   I didn't expect to see you.

You say nothing.

Old lady   I'm sure you didn't think you'd find me here, sitting up like this.

You frown.

Old lady   Lying down I was until they came and said I should get up and sit in the chair again. I couldn't. Not get up, I said. And they said, of course you must, and they propped me here. Left me.

I was watching you for a long time. You and that girl.

You   Melinda.

Old lady   Why is she in uniform? Did you pick her up? You picked her up, didn't you? Disgusting, never happened when I was young.

They said, you'll be all right here, Mrs Donkins. Silly, they are. Always getting my name wrong. Johnkins, I said, not Don, John, with a J, Johnkins. But they never learn. That's all right, Mrs Donkins, you sit here in the window and I'll leave your stick by the side so you'se can get up when you want. How can I get up? I can't walk no more. Look at me.

You look.

Oooh, I said. By the window. I am lucky. But what is there to look at, I said, I mean it's not

57

as if this was the High Street, is it? No-one. Until you came along.

With that girl of yours.

She's taller than you are. Did you know that? I could see that, and it isn't because of her shoes. I could see that too. I take a good note of what goes on.

Why is she in uniform?

You look at the closed door.

I'm not contagious, you know.

You turn back to her.

And it was me told them to shut the door. Don't want them listening. Always listening they are. To everything I say. You go and open it and look outside. You'll hear them scuttling away like mice. They live in holes, they do, but we don't have mice in this house. Them. They think I'm gone, you see, and they're waiting for me. That's why they're always listening. Every word I say.

Now you just come a little closer. Don't want them hearing me all the time.

The carpet is a rich pattern of shapes and textures. Her face is lined and shrunken from its former fullness, maybe her teeth are still her own, her hair is white and straightly thin, her skin has lost the translucence of youth. Her fingers curl like spiders legs over the edges of the frame of the chair. She is smiling at you and her feet shuffle in a mirror of your own hesitant movements. In the dim light of the past you sense a fascination. Maybe she has something of value to tell you.

I'm going to die.

Whatever do you say? You hope it is nice where she's going. Send her a postcard. Where is this place of myths and legends?

She is whispering again so you move forward, close enough to touch the chair but not yet her frail body and for a while there is silence. Nothing happens in the room until you become acutely aware of a clock ticking. It must be a small clock, a wristwatch even. It has a regularity, a normality, and as you stand there next to her worn seat, smelling the age of her skirt, the beat becomes more insistent as of a ratchet being forced forwards. It is a ratchet, you know that, but now the machine dominates the space. It is time marching relentlessly onwards, time proclaimed by human ingenuity which sees the sun going down at the end of each day and the memories of spring and autumn, the waxing and waning of the moon. What work of hands is this, who fashioned metal into ornament that now tyrannises you and her? The tiny wristwatch crashes thunderously each revolving second. Perpetual motion never letting the present stay for one minute longer. Satan is coming to claim his goods. The diamonds on the face of the watch, the gold surrounding its silvered hands, he gave them in promise of your soul, your soul and hers.

> I don't know why they put me in the window. There's nothing to see out there. No-one ever walks down this street, except you and your girl. Why is she in uniform?
>
> Well, don't you worry about that because I can guess, I've seen enough in my lifetime. More than them, the listening, snivelling brutes. They grip me so hard, my arms are all bruised.

I wasn't born here, you know. Far away,now, your little mother. Like she was tossed up in a basket over the moon and never came back. And she never did clean off the cobwebs.

Why don't you sit down? There's plenty of chairs. You look un-tidy like that standing on the carpet. Sit down. I won't keep you long, I haven't got long. I've been a long time here, longer than you imagine, longer than them. I don't hate them, I just wish they wouldn't listen so much. But you can listen, you're good, you are. Yes, you pull up that chair and come and sit next to me. We can look out of the window together. It's a long time till teatime. Nice tea.

The chair is old and small.

They say it was country when I was little. Did I say my mother was little?

You nod.

She wasn't. I'm a liar. She was big, big she was, she could hold me in her arms and I could never see nothing except her, and she was so gentle, she never made a mark on me. See that?

She shows you her leg.

That's where she caught me with the saucepan. Full it was. Hot custard. And I didn't get anything to eat that night.

She laughs, a high girlish laugh, as if the room were filled with pixies that peer out of pots and jars, from behind the picture rails and in the pages of books.

I don't like this room, it's dirty. And it's small. There isn't enough room in here and they've painted the ceiling. It's not like it was, we had ceilings high and big like clouds.

I wonder where my brother is. He said he would come. He's dead, you know. They said he was missing but I know he's dead. It was a long time ago. Come in the night.

She starts singing, a song that may have words but none that you can understand. She sings softly with a delicate poignancy in the only way she can express her deep longing. You would join in, your voice an octave lower, adding a note of solemnity, for you too are about to grieve with her for the times that are gone.

The song is over.

A smile flits over her loosely hanging jaw.

> *Come in the night*
> *and play by my side with me*
> *Sit in the light*
> *and we'll journey till ever be*
> *Hold to me tight*
> *and the work will be done*
>
> *Faith in my sight*
> *for the days are not gone*
>
> *Come in the night*
> *and whisper your dreams to me*
> *I have the might*
> *to go onward in destiny*
> *Do not take fright*
> *for the darkness will go*
> *Give me your plight*
> *Let the world be just so.*

Outside in the street, lamps begin to glow and the orange sodium light makes patterns on the wallpaper.

I'll tell you why she's in uniform. It's because you think you love her, but you don't. All you want from her is her body. Well, it won't do. A woman needs more than that from a man. Her body is the last preciousness, it's her refuge. And there you go. In and out and it's all done. Don't look at me like that. Do you think I haven't lived? I've enjoyed myself just as anyone but I always knew.

Her smile grows broad and fades.

He had dark hair, not like Percival. And he never knew, at least, he never said he did. You know, when it came to the end there wasn't much left. We used to lie there together side by side and that could have been it, but desire can't be satisfied, not once and for ever, it goes on and on.

Why don't you turn the light on? It's miserable sitting here with them streetlamps shining in. We don't have to pay for it, you know. Just switch it on and there it is. Bright again.

When you return to the chair you look at her face.

You don't say much, do you? What's your name? You have got a name, everybody has a name, even if they keep it a secret. I remember when we used to play behind the sheds, we had a secret society. The only witnesses were the dolls and if they told anyone they would have their faces pushed into the mud, so they never said another word unless we asked them. I don't know why I'm telling you this. Maybe, your face is honest.

Are you in trouble? It's an awful thing when you get a girl pregnant. You don't know where to turn and you're sure you'll be spurned and you worry about losing her and then there's that awful pride in your child. Your child. It won't do, it won't be your child for long, it'll grow up just like any other and become a person and end up like me, sitting in a chair by the window with no-one to look at and no-one to talk to and people listening all the time.

There's somebody coming!

You look round. The door is still. The street beyond the lace is dark.

I've still got my doll. They tried hard to take it away from me, but I wouldn't let them. Heartless they are, they listen to everything I say and they don't know nothing. They don't know who they're talking to. I'm not a sack of potatoes and I've still got legs even if I can't walk. How do they know anything about me? They've never asked me. All they know is, I'm old, older than them. Young scallywags. But I was the same as them. And you. We got into scrapes, we was rebels, but we did it different. And I've still got my doll.

The door opens.

Nurse   Are you all right, Mrs Donkins?

And before she has time to protest at the misuse of her name or to affirm that at this moment she has no wants that the nurse can satisfy, the nurse has vanished into the flights of stairs. Whether up or down you do not know, you only know that the stairs continue in both directions to floors unknown, to territories inhabited by memories

63

which have yet to be brought into the light, dim though it is, of this lukewarm sitting room. You look down at the carpet. Turkey red. The room is really quite well furnished. The old lady's chair, Mrs Donkins, or Mrs Johnkins, firm, is worn at the edges, she has sat there, placed so that she is in the room and set with a view onto the street. Things must happen in the street, houses are lived in, there may be empty properties, a flat waiting for new occupants, a room vacated but they are houses, not offices, nor hotels. It's possible that there are shops or, if not shops, then merchants who come past in the hope of selling, peddlers of salvation, the window cleaner, meter readers, telephone repairmen, plumbers, the odd spot of carpentry, men on the roof. The street is teeming with life; only you and she haven't seen what life is. What were you wanting? The photos of childhood to be forever playing in the thoroughfare?

They have silver frames. The pictures show a girl with flowing curls holding a spoon, and a tender mother looking down from a face that is lined with concern. It is a cold day, they have coats on and boots done up to the ankles. Another picture of a man, elegant, suave, posing for the photographer. Perhaps he was proud of his image. The table is polished, the fruit in the bowl is fresh, the lampshade is old, but it is free from dust. Whoever lives here is proud also, keeps the place pleasant. This is Mrs Johnkins' sitting room, the room where she sits to end her days, too tired to work, waiting for peace to arrive which it already has but like the life in the street it has come unnoticed. You wonder about Mrs Johnkins' life, what truth she saw, in simple forms, what she read in the books that fill the shelves, what she saw in the pictures, the landscapes on the walls, the faded photographs on the mantle. The wallpaper is modern.

Her face is a bit worn now, like yours, only yours is wrinkled and hers is rubbed smooth.

Old lady   Why don't you tell me about yourself now, I've been talking too much.

There is too much pain for her to continue, the memory of her doll, which is packed in a suitcase, a heavy trunk, has prompted feelings of loss, those parts of your body which no-one can ever regain, people you loved, places you roamed in, times relentlessly gone, all that you have, cut.

Old lady   My stick.

She bangs it hard on the floor and within seconds you hear the sound of feet racing up the staircase. The door flies open and the nurse stands for instructions.

Old lady   When is tea ready?

The nurse is apologetic.

Old lady   And my friend is staying, so make sure there is enough for two.

    Silly thing.

She drops the stick.

    No, you stay as long as you like. I keep a good house and there's always food in the cupboard. I may not be able to move around but I know what there is. Silly thing, getting my name wrong. Come on, don't be so hesitant.

You begin.

    I don't want to know where you live, I want to know how. I've lived in more places than you have and I tell you it doesn't matter. Not a bit. I've been here too long in this long street, but I still want to see and they put me in the chair like this on purpose, you know, so I can't see. I remember running all the way, I was top of the class for running. I could run faster than all of them.

There is silence.

No. You tell me about yourself, who you think you are. I know who I am and then I forget. Sometimes I sit here and I'm sewing away at uniforms, putting zips in trousers. Those silly girls couldn't do it, so they gave them all to me and I did them. I was the tops, you know, I did all the zips and when I'd done the zips I did pockets and waistbands and when I'd done them I did buttons and frills. Careless they were, leaving bits of the hems, cutting the material short, skimping, they gave them to me to bind so they wouldn't fray. I'm not boasting, I just knew my job. If the pattern said two yards I could always get it out of less. Trousers, thousands of trousers. We never knew who were they for, not their names or where they were, just trousers for the men, out in the battlefields shooting their guns. It never bothered me, I used to sleep in my bed. Wouldn't catch me going down in the shelters, all smelly. Yes, fetid they were, from the sweat. But I wasn't frightened of silly things flying in the sky.

You look together out into the street but it is too dark to see what is in the sky and the streetlamps glare back at you.

I was out when the bomb fell. It wasn't there when I got back, the house, my room a heap in the house and all I found was a book. Must have been flung out by the blast, landed on the path by the fishpond.

She bangs her stick hard on the floor but this time it is not answered; the house remains still in the glowing orange light of memories.

No tea today.

She sighs. Feelings waft like smells occasionally picked up by nostrils, but more often passing undetected like undersea currents which produce climates, deserts and rainforests, winters without snow and summers without sun. You and the old woman are as spirits tossed on the waves of the unconscious, paddling on the surface of the ocean while the great surges of life carry you to your separate destinations. You remember the time when you were swept out to sea. You were happy then, to be part of the great current of life. Only when you were dragged back to the dry shoreline did your tears run, frustrated in your intentions, caught by the expression of their fear, held in their arms as if in a prison, escape was a distant prospect, mollified only by sweets and smiles.

Won't be the first time I've gone without my tea.

The door opens to admit the nurse bearing a tray with tea laid out on it; tea for two.

What about his lady friend? There's more than just the two of us you know.

She stretches out a fragile hand and begins to pour the tea. She assumes you take milk, she assumes you take sugar, she passes you without asking a plate on which she has put two biscuits. Why do you say nothing? You hate sweet tea, but you eat and drink in silence as the door closes.

He's gone now, you know, gone a long time, and he won't return. He was a good man, Percy. Patient. Well, he had to be with me. His hair all grey and mostly not at all and I'm not the one responsible, don't you go thinking that about me, he had his own share, saint or no saint, he could sin as hard as anyone.

Turns us all grey in the end.

Her hand reaches for another biscuit which she munches mechanically, ruminating on her life with Percy and others unnamed.

I'm proud! Do you know that? Proud that I've still got my own hair and my own teeth. Grey and yellow.

Her shrill laugh fills the air. It is the laughter of the gods when they realise that for all the faults of creation life is bearable and people are alive.

Do you love your girl? Do you love your girl with the uniform? It won't do. No, shake your head if you like, but it won't do, not loving won't, because in the end one or other will have to let go. Like Percy, he moved on and here I am staring out the window waiting for him to come home. Which he won't.

And she smiles broadly, remembering the wonderful loving with Percy, the glorious loving in his arms and the intertwining of their naked bodies when youth gave them energy, boundless energy to people the earth with their progeny brought forth out of loving, too much loving. The shrillness has cracked a glass.

Will you do something for me? Will you promise me to go on loving no matter what I say, to keep loving to the end of your days?

Because there isn't any other way, you know. Oh, I know I talk rubbish, but it isn't really rubbish, it just comes out the wrong way. I'm old and I've got so much to tell you. I know where to begin, only not where to end. I will end, you know? One day, they won't wheel me in here anymore to sit at the window because one day I won't be here to look out of the window.

She's still there your girl, your girl in the uniform. She's waiting for you and we've finished the tea. Not left her any tea. Those silly girls, I told them there was more than just the two of us, but they never listen, never listen to me. Yes, Mrs Donkins. All right, Mrs Donkins. I get so cross. I bang my stick, I could bang it through their silly heads but I haven't the strength, not anymore, so you keep on loving and never let go, although you'll have to let go one day, like me, you'll have to let go and not know and be all alone, staring out through a different window onto a different world.

And I will be laughing then, because they won't be listening to me anymore. I'll be dead. Dead, that's what I'll be, dead to their world and this silly window and this long dead street and the wheel chairs and the sticks and the tea in the wrong pot and them not answering when I call and the dreams I have in the night. Dead. At last.

She shuts her eyes, nodding her head violently so that the cup rattles and you reach out to save the cup, but the energy catches you so that your arm begins to vibrate in the same rhythm. Perhaps this is the rattle of death, come to claim his next client, perhaps he has your name on his list, ready to take you into the world from which no-one returns. You gasp out loud and pull your arm back.

You would prefer to return to the street to hold Melinda by the hand, but you will stay longer at the side of Mrs Johnkins, whose tale you are beginning to hear. You could relinquish the old lady to her seat by the window; she would be unlikely to notice as you slip quietly across the red Turkey carpet. One, two or three cups on the tray. Maybe she has not been talking to you, only muttering into the air of the room or through the glass panes into the empty street, hoping for a friendly ear.

You shut your eyes. Observe the turmoil in your centre. Become aware of the terror that has gripped you. What honour is this, what respect for a dying woman? Now you know that she is the image of your mother, she who gave you sustenance at her breast, who watched you grow, played with you, encouraged you, sent you to learn, punished you according to her laws, stood silently by your rebellion and watched you leave her house.

Whose turn is it to weep for the losses of the past?

You stay in the soft light of the room, close the curtains, sit quietly in the chair, drink sugar sweetened tea, and listen.

> He had a way with me, with women, you know. He used to charm us into thinking he would be just what we needed. He did it to me and he thought I never knew, but I loved him for all of him. I loved him for his giddy ways, jumping up to take me off to the theatre. Always booked the best seats, couldn't make do with the cheapest.

70

And cross he got. When I didn't wear my best.

Now you go ask your girl down there what she has in her wardrobe. She'll surprise you. She'll take off her uniform and underneath there she'll stand in the most beautiful dress you've ever seen.

Ooh, you're wicked, thinking thoughts like that. Same as him, fondling and then declaring he meant nothing by it. But I understood him, I understood when he came home worn out, exhausted by fantasies. Poor Percy.

I don't know why I say he was poor. He had plenty of money. Well, no, to be honest, he thought he did. Funny that. Most folks always think they haven't got enough but not Percy. Always generous he was, splashing his money around like his wallet would never be empty. But in the end it was. Empty. Like him. Like you. Empty. Nothing more except to look out of the window up and down the street where no-one walks.

I wondered why you two were walking down this street. First time in ages that I've seen anyone walk.

She sits straight up.

Now, will you tell her and if you will, what will you say? Running away? Blind leading the blind? Ambling until you were lost?

I used to walk!

I used to be able to walk, to run, to dance, to move all as I desired! I did!

71

She slams her stick onto the floor. And you jump at her sudden anger. The room is filled with noise and anxiety. Feet crisscross the carpet, the shade of the lamp is bustled by lights being switched on so that faces can peer more intently into hers but she snatches her hand away.

> Of course, I'm all right. Leave me alone, won't you!

The nurse leaves, frightened by her efforts to preserve life, and she takes with her the calmness of the room. Mrs Johnkins broods, her anger stuffed inside like a pillow shaken so that the feathers expand so far and no further.

You were interested in what she was saying. But she is captured by the stiff wooden arms of her chair. She glares at you as if you were a policeman come to interrogate her life away. She turns her head back to the window.

> Go away now.

Chapter 7

MELINDA

In the street, a bus, your home
You & Melinda

You come down the steps from the front door. Shiny black paint. Brass letter box. Brass numbers. No 39. Portico. Marble steps. You look briefly into the area. Clean swept. Railings.

Melinda is waiting for you patiently. She is relaxed.

You Oh, I'm so glad you're still here. I thought you might have gone by now, I was quite a long time upstairs.

Melinda Who was she?

You Mrs Donkins.

Melinda How did you know her?

You Oh, no, not a D, Mrs Johnkins. She looked after me when I was little. She was like a mother to me. I used to go and see her once or twice a year. When I was younger it was every week. Then times changed. I had things to do. Got out of the habit. And then sometimes I nearly forgot altogether. So it was good to go up and see her.

Melinda How was she?

You I'm not sure she recognised me, not fully. It was a while ago. She is being looked after. That's a cruel fate. In your prime you're the carer, the one who does the looking after, feeding, washing, attending to all your needs. And then, poof! You end up parked in a chair you can't get out of, stuck beside a window that you don't want to look out of, having to bang your stick on the floor to get a cup of tea.

Melinda   Sad.

You   I thought you would come upstairs. She had three cups ready.

Melinda   I didn't know I was invited.

You   Funny, how everything was old. The cups, the carpet, the wallpaper, the pictures. All old and past it. Must have been right in fashion when she bought them. All old now, though.

Melinda   Yes.

You   Do you know where we are?

Melinda   No. Beltane Street? Medlock Road? I haven't a clue how we got here. Did you know we were coming here?

You   No, I thought you did. That's why I went up to see her.

Melinda   You're lying aren't you? You wouldn't forget someone's name if they'd looked after you when you were little. And you wouldn't call her Mrs Johnkins. She'd have a nice name. Mum or Ma. Or Betty.

You don't reply. It is a lie. Even you don't know. You laugh. It's hollow. You are embarrassed. How to get out of it? Blue serge. You wonder if she's naked underneath, like the matron at the zoo.

You   Why are you in uniform?

Melinda   Sorry?

You   Well, that blue serge you're wearing. It looks like it's a uniform. It looks like you belong to an organisation.

Melinda	I do.
You	So, that's why you're in uniform!
Melinda	No, that's not quite the way it is.

Oh God. This is going to get complicated. Again. First the bird is dead. Then it's flying off somewhere. Then the inspector. You bet he's not genuine. Oh no, you think he must be. He didn't half smash your face on the floor. God, that hurt. Now Melinda is in uniform and she's not and she belongs to an organisation and she doesn't. How are you going to extricate yourselves? Time will tell. That's what they say, but you're not sure time does always tell. Because the problem with time is that you tend to forget what the question was so that by the time time has told you haven't a clue what the answer is supposed to mean. Oh well.

Melinda	How on earth did we get here?
You	By walking.
Melinda	Oh, do you have to take everything so literally?
You	Yes, there isn't any other way. Everybody takes everything literally. Especially when it's meant to be a story, a metaphor. You do, I do, everybody. And if they can ascribe divine provenance it's even better. God said this, God said that. Wonderful. All religion is like that, you know. Make up a rule, no matter how preposterous; say God told you; and hey presto, it's the truth. Absolute magic. No basis in fact or reality and, if you threaten to expose the fallacy, they turn straight back on you and say that's just it, God is the reality and before you know it you're stuck in one hell of a conundrum trying to figure out how something

which patently isn't true is accepted by millions as gospel truth. Literally.

Melinda sighs.

You	So when I met you at the zoo were you working for the zoo?
Melinda	No.
You	What do you mean, no?
Melinda	You didn't meet me. I appeared.
You	Isn't that the same?
Melinda	No. it's not the same because if it were a meeting it might imply that you had some idea of who I was before the encounter. Whereas, you haven't a clue who I am or what I do or why. Do you?

Now, it's your turn to sigh.

Melinda	You haven't answered my question. Why did you lie about Mrs whatever? Being your mother?
You	She wasn't my mother.
Melinda	I know that. So why did you tell me something purely fabricated? Made up? A lie?
You	Can we move on, please?
Melinda	You're not going to say anything, are you? You probably don't know yourself, do you?
You	No.
Melinda	You're a right mystery.
You	I know.
Melinda	You know?
You	No, I don't know. That's the problem. I don't know who I am. I don't know who you are. I don't know why that police bloke is so angry

with me. I don't know why I went upstairs to Mrs Donkins. I don't know who I am.

You hold her hand. She is kind, her hand feels warm. You are walking away from No 39. The plane trees are coming into leaf. You step carefully past a pile of dog poo. You have no idea where you are going and you don't think Melinda has either. Maybe it will all become clear. For now you keep walking. Turning a corner, there's a bus stop. No 39. Is it a coincidence? Does it have some meaning? What can 39 have to do with anything. You wait. Not long. A bus appears, stops, you get on, show your bus passes, you both have one. The bus drives off. You go up the stairs. Still not knowing the destination of the bus, or of the two of you. Perhaps Melinda is an employee of the bus company. Her jacket looks as though it could be. She smiles at you. The bus slows to a stop.

You   Come on, this is us.

Melinda   Oh.

You are standing on the pavement, still not knowing where you are or what you're doing there, with this woman you've only met a couple of hours ago. At least you know her name and you wouldn't be surprised if she was 39 years old. Though you would be surprised but then you've never been very good at people's ages. You make them twenty years younger than they are. Or twenty years older. Thank heavens you're too polite to ask her directly. Or too shy more like. You smile.

Melinda   OK, where are we then?

You're taken aback. You thought she was taking you and now it turns out you're taking her.

You   Me?

Melinda   Yes. This is your journey. Not mine.

You are thrown back. No, it can't be to the beginning. So where to start. It has to be the beginning because that is where it starts. It is the beginning of your journey. It is what brought you to this place.

Ah, this place. You stop musing and open your eyes. You see exactly where you are. How you didn't recognise it straight away, you don't know. These last few hours have been a blur. That copper smashing your face on the floor. The bun. It wasn't a stone. You ate some of it.

You turn to cross over the street. Here you are. Home.

You   Are you coming in with me?

Melinda   No, not today, it's probably best.

You're disappointed. You like her company and it's not that you want sex with her, though, of course, that is exactly what you want. Dick was right, you're a prick.

You   Oh.

You open the door. It smells familiar. It's your smell. But it feels like a long time since you were here. Yet, surely it was only this morning when you left. Or was it longer ago? Is it possible that you've been away for a long time. That the time you've been experiencing hasn't been running according to any convention. Have the hands on the clock been standing still? Have they been going round so fast it's a blur. The time between two seconds is more than a second; it is infinite. The time between aeons passes in a trice. You've been here before. You know you have, you remember the smell. It is your smell so it must be where you belong or perhaps you don't belong anywhere. Perhaps you are just one of a million or a billion to roam the earth in search of a place to call your own, when the reality is that the earth owns you and not the other way around. You don't have a right to own anywhere. Your place is anywhere and nowhere and everywhere. Just like time, place is not specific. Space like time is as vast as you can imagine and so tight there isn't any room for anything let alone you. All at the same time. Is it time or is it space? So intimately connected; without space there is no time; without time there is no space. Without movement neither. Does movement give rise to existence. Is there nothing if it does not move? Does the whole universe depend purely on change? Without change does it collapse into a black hole of infinite nothingness, where there is no time and no space.

You switch on the light. That's better. You can see now. Same carpet. Same coats hanging on the pegs. Same grubby wallpaper. Same smell. Her picture. The hall table. Still got the keys lying there.

The door slams. You jump.

Melinda stands for a while on the pavement looking into the hallway. When the door shuts, she turns to go when she realises this person she's been befriending… is that the right word, accompanying, assisting, no it's more than that, it must be befriending. No that suggests she isn't really interested in knowing you, that she only wants to make you feel less alone, that when you feel good, good enough, she'll say goodbye, she'll leave you. She knows deep in her heart she has feelings for you. She hasn't been able to make those feelings fully conscious but her conscious mind's thought of turning away to continue whatever she was doing earlier this morning is unable to make her feet obey.

She stands. She is looking at the door. She needs to know you. She wants more than that. Her juices. Oh god. Why did she say no? She held your hand. Oh god. This is intolerable. To come or to go. To go or to stay. Quiet.

You're not like anyone she's ever met before. What harm would it be?

There's a doorbell. She doesn't want to ring the bell, that would be too soon after saying she won't come in. She goes to the front step. There are five bells. Labels beside the bells but they aren't clear. She gets closer. The labels are blank.

Melinda   How inconsiderate.

She rings one of the bells. You open the door. You're not surprised, just pleased. She grins.

You   Hello.

Melinda   I changed my mind. I hope you don't mind.

You   Not at all.

Melinda takes off her blue serge jacket. A big disappointment, she isn't naked underneath. Perhaps you had entertained thoughts that she was a... but you daren't even whisper the word to yourself. You really are a prick. Your inner desires are straining and your shadow is raring to go and still you push them away.

There is a long pause. You know you must offer her a coffee or something but you really want to ask her to go upstairs with you.

You   Would you like a drink?

Melinda   Yes, please, that would be nice.

Missed opportunity. Blast. You were hoping she'd ask if there wasn't something more important. But, of course, she doesn't, she's not a mind reader.

You do nothing. She is holding her jacket. You take it from her and hang it over a newel post. You do nothing.

Melinda   It's been quite a day, hasn't it?

You   Uh huh.

Melinda   Go and make some coffee and I'll tell you what I think we should do.

You go into the kitchen. Kettle. Water. Coffee jar. Empty. Cupboard. New jar. Silver foil. Dig finger nail into it. Tear it off. Cups. Mugs. Other cupboard. Sugar. Does she take sugar. Offer it. Milk. Fridge. Amazing. Milk. Kettle boiled. Table. Chairs. The coffee tastes bitter and it's too hot.

Melinda   Are you ready?

Your eyes light up.

You   Yes.

Melinda   You've got to go back to the bakery.

You   What?

Melinda   Get there before the inspector.

You   What?

Melinda   Don't you realise that's what he's doing?

You   No.

Melinda   Well, I can't be absolutely sure but I do know him. You'll have to forestall him if he finds out what you've done, he'll pursue you until he's got you in prison for murder.

You   Attempted murder.

Melinda   OK. Attempted.

You   Which it wasn't.

Melinda   Wasn't what?

You   Attempted. Not that and not for actual either. And besides it was only a bloody bird. And I didn't even see it eat anything before it fell off its perch. Stupid bird. Just play acting. Did you see it eat the bun?

Melinda   No.

You	So why are you so interested?
Melinda	I saw the cockatoo lying on the ground. And I saw the inspector approaching. And I thought, oh dear, this is bad news. So I thought I'd try to help.
You	Thank you.
Melinda	Oh, nothing to thank. It's what I do.
You	Why? Have you done it before? Helping people you've never met in your life. I mean, you don't know me, do you? I mean, what?
Melinda	Do you remember, you asked what sort of organisation I belong to. You asked me why I'm in uniform.
You	Yes.
Melinda	So, this it. This is the organisation.
You	What?
Melinda	I'll tell you later. We're using up valuable time. We need to get going.
You	We can't.
Melinda	How? We can't get going?
You	No, it's not that. We could get going all right but I wouldn't know which way. I did buy the bun. And it was a bun. It wasn't a stone, I don't care what that copper thinks, there was nothing wrong with it. I just didn't eat it all. And I thought the bird might like some.
Melinda	So?
You	The fact is, Melinda, I haven't a clue where the bakery is. Or was? I know it was there when I bought the bun. And I paid for it. All proper. She gave me the change. I can show you. But the bakery. I don't know where it is. It might

not even be there anymore. It might have appeared because I was hungry and wanted a bite to eat.

Melinda   So, why didn't you eat all of it?

You   Don't know. Satisfied with a couple of bites, perhaps. It tasted all right. Sweet, you know. Chelsea bun. That's all. But where I bought it?

Melinda   And you're hoping Inspector Daks won't find it because you don't know where it is.

You   I'm not bothered about him.

You are lying. He smashed your face on the floor and you certainly don't want that again. But at the same time you don't want to be dragged round the city by Melinda looking for a stupid bakery which probably doesn't exist. Might never have existed. Oh, no, on second thoughts, you did buy the bun, so it must have been in a shop of some sort, maybe a bakery. But a ruddy goose chase.

Cockatoo whistles.

You look out of the window.

You   Oh, all right then.

Melinda   Good.

You   Where to start?

Melinda   At the front door. That's the normal place. And decide whether to turn left or right.

You stare out of the window.

You   What about the back door?

Melinda   Is there a gate out of the garden?

You   No.

Melinda   So, going into the city via the back door of this house which leads into a garden, maximum 30 feet, with no other exit, except to return into the house. It's not ideal.

You   No, but it's more interesting.

Melinda   More interesting?

You   Yes. There's plenty in the garden I've never fully explored. We could find something.

Melinda   But not a bakery.

You   True. We'd better go out the front door, then.

You clear the mugs away, leave the stain from the spoon, fetch Melinda's jacket, open the front door. A bus passes. Melinda joins you.

Melinda   Which way then?

You   Well, the Zoo is that way and.

You stop abruptly.

Melinda   What?

Did you go into the Zoo? Are you sure it was you? You don't remember how you got into the Zoo. But you must have been there because that's where you met Melinda, where the bird toppled off its perch, where Daks smashed your face in the guardhouse. God, that hurt. You show your face to Melinda.

Melinda   Is it bleeding?

You   No.

Melinda   This way then.

You follow her.

Cockatoo is surprised.

Chapter 8
FLIGHT

In the square
Cockatoo, Nelson, Inspector Daks, Dick

Inspector William Daks, he the badger of the Metropolitan Police is planning to go snouting. A shop cannot exist at one time and disappear the next. Such is not acceptable to the logical mind. If such does exist, then he needs a complete and total and full explanation as to how such a phenom... how such a... well anyway how anything of that sort or kind could occur. And that's enough long words. From now on he's going to use nothing more than two whatsits and certainly none of your foreign muck, jargon, slang, rhyming or not.

Cockatoo takes notice.

You might be led into thinking that Cockatoo is in some way going to assist Inspector Daks but you'd be incredibly wrong, not that there is anything to believe in the first place.

Cockatoo has his own business to attend to. First of all to climb down from his mighty perch. He takes a last look around, that is as far as he is able with his feet firmly sculpted into the stone of the hero's hat. With a bit of effort he can pick out the landmarks. Tower, dome, smaller dome, taller tower. Colonnade. Fountains. Cross on top of spire. Second cross on top of smaller tower. Statue more like. Corner house. Serving tea. Bus stop. Those pesky starlings not to mention the plague of pigeons squawking and the sparrows. So much going on. He peers. In the distance more towers. More landmarks but too far away to distinguish from the haze of smoke, fumes, air conditioners' puffs, chestnut sellers' heat. No hang on there, not yet, that comes much later in the year. This is springtime. And of course, crowds of people lolling, strolling, flopping, flipping, lounging, scrounging, sipping, kipping, staring, sharing, ice cream, peanuts, toffee, apples, coffee, chocolate, wrapped in silver, paper bags, cornets, cardboard beakers.

Cockatoo extricates his feet, flaps his wings, spreads his gorgeous white tail feathers, plumes his crest of gold. And nothing happens.

Cockatoo   Damn!
          Blast!

Nelson   Now watch it young fellow. I can hear everything you say.

Cockatoo   What?

Nelson   Exactly, what?
          You think because I'm just a piece of old stone, painted black, I don't have feelings and sensations. Well, my feathery flummery friend, I do.

Cockatoo   Whoops. Sorry.

Nelson   Sorry! You'll be even more sorry when I release you and you find yourself unattached, unanchored.

Cockatoo   So that's it, is it?

Nelson   Indeed it is.

Cockatoo   You mean, before I can go, I've got to do something for you, your honour.

Nelson   Not honour. Can't stand it. It's bad enough being gawped at without being insulted.

Cockatoo	Oh, come on, surely an honour is an honour. Just because you'd prefer to be an ordinary seaman you can't really complain. I mean after all, what do you think this country would have become if you hadn't achieved your magnificent feats. Heroic, I'd even say.
Nelson	Heroic be damned, blast you. Flukes of history. The other feller made worse mistakes than me. And what have I got to show for it? An eyepatch and my bloody arm in a sling. Really humiliating. I mean, how am I going to offer a proper salute? Or put the silly telescope, wrong end, to my face to see what the enemy is up to?
Cockatoo	Yes, I see what you're up against. Maybe that's why they put me up here with you. To offer you sight into the distance.
Nelson	And a fat lot of good that did me, eh? Dead me, dead bird.

Flukes they were. Got shot at and that was the end of it. Except when the clouds cleared I saw he was sinking faster than we were. Turned tail before you could even spit out the words.

Gotcha! No, got me, fuck you. |
Cockatoo	I wish I'd been there.
Nelson	Really? Do you have any idea what war is about. It's a bloody awful business and I mean bloody. Blood everywhere. Stinks, screams, writhing, smell of powder, stench of sweat. Fear ruling the air and the waves. None of this bravery. More cowardice I'd say. You should have seen the men.
Cockatoo	Well, I wish I had.

Nelson	I hope you don't mean that.
Cockatoo	Yes, I do. I'd have gotten a much better perspective. Even your man up in the crow's nest.
Nelson	You bloody fool. He couldn't see anything. Whatever makes you think you could have seen. What sort of height were you going to fly at? Above the acrid clouds. Not a chance. In the clouds, get your stupid beak stinging with the acid? You'd have come down as quick as you could and you'd have ended up in the hail of shot with cannonballs whizzing round your own little balls.
Cockatoo	Who are you calling little?
Nelson	Oh come on. Puny.
Cockatoo	All right, I give in.
Nelson	Right. And before we go any further, no more heroes. Not now. Not never. We'll be a lot better off if everybody who thought they could, took one little step back and realised, in fact, they couldn't. Not a hope in hell chance. And if they did, like me by a fluke, they'd be condemned for a life of death stuck on a wretched fluted column so high they'd never get their feet on the ground anymore.
Cockatoo	So. Rant over?
Nelson	Rant over.
Cockatoo	Sure?
Nelson	No.

Inspector Bill Daks hears a commotion above him. He is intrigued.

Nelson	And anyway, it's called a crow's nest because no intelligent bird would be so stupid to sit up there on top of the mast.
Cockatoo	Exactly, you see, that means you know I'm not stupid.
Nelson	Yes, you are. Totally.

Daks strains his ear, but the roar of the traffic is louder. All he can see is the familiar statue, but too high up to be able to see clearly. Or hear.

He returns to the job in hand. Did you or did you not sell a stone baked Chelsea bun? Or to rephrase that, a baked stone Chelsea bun? A Chelsea stone bun baked? A bun of stone baked in Chelsea?

Yes! Triumph! That must be where the bakery is. Or was. Is. Shops don't disappear. They tend to stay where they are. Why even hesitate. They don't just tend, they do. No doubt about it. Triumph Street, Chelsea. Deduction pays off. Handsome.

Cockatoo clips his shoulder.

Daks	What on earth was that?
Cockatoo	Nothing. I'm in the sky.
Daks	Clever Dick.
Dick	What? Did you want me?

Dick strolls past with the tripod over his shoulder. Daks takes out his handkerchief. Sees Dick.

Daks	Excuse me, young man, can I see your A to Z?
Dick	My what?
Daks	Your A to Z.

Daks blows his nose.

Dick	You've got a nerve. In broad daylight! In the middle of a public square.

Dick leaves.

Daks No, I don't think it's a square. More of a street, a road. Called Triumph. Anyway it's a fair distance from here. As the crow flies. Or whatever that bird is. Practically flew into my face. Feather right up my nose.

Cockatoo I am not a crow.

Daks No, true. No self-respecting crow would look anything like you. For a start, crows are black and you are distinctly of a white colour. Ridiculous bird.

Cockatoo Laugh you may. Shall I show you the direction?

Daks That would be very kind, thank you.

Cockatoo It's over there.

Daks Is that it? You just point?

Cockatoo Yes. I said I'd show you the direction. I didn't say I'd take you there or give you the directions, plural.

Daks True. But it's a bit off to take things that literally.

Cockatoo Is it? In any case your powers of deduction leave much to be questioned. To call a bun by the name of a place doesn't necessarily mean it has to be made in that place.

Daks Yes it does. Cornish pasty. Bakewell pie. Bath bun. Harrogate teacake.

Cockatoo Harrogate teacake? Where did you make that one up from?

Daks I didn't. I bought one there.

Cockatoo You bought a teacake in Harrogate and so that's what you called it?

Daks	Yes, perfectly reasonable and logical.
Cockatoo	Same thing.
Daks	What?
Cockatoo	Reasonable and logical. Doesn't mean either are right.
Daks	Well, think what you like. Show me again the way to Chelsea.
Cockatoo	That way.
Daks	Very helpful. Straight through a building.
Cockatoo	I'm a bird. I can't help it if you're a man on two legs who can't fly.

Inspector Daks walks away.

Cockatoo is alone.

Not quite. The statue hasn't moved.

Cockatoo bends double.

Cockatoo	I know they're little. But I must just have a check to see if they're there at all. I might have got it completely wrong. Puny indeed.
Nelson	Whatever do you think you're doing? This is a public square for heaven's sake.
Cockatoo	Oh! Does heaven require squares to be public? Or squares to be at all? In order for heaven to be in right ordering.
Nelson	Yes. Emphatically so.
Cockatoo	And I now know emphatically which gender I am. Thank you. I'm off.
Nelson	That's it. Left me on my own again. Nothing to ward off the pigeons. Make do with some representative feathers. Not the same though. Who am I going to talk to? Same old sky, clouds, rain sweeping down, sun, fog, church

bells, bloody pigeons, starlings all over the place.

Cockatoo is miles away.

Chapter 9
DEAD

The street

You, a Road Sweeper, Melinda

The old lady died during the night. It was neither sudden nor unexpected; she slipped into a different world and her spirit left her body, tired, disabled, scarred. Someone came to tell you, someone who slipped into your life, gave you the message and slipped out again before you had time to comprehend the full import. "Cecile is dead", they said. They were a plural person. "Cecile", you said, "Cecile is French". And you might have continued but they were no longer within earshot. Off into the mist of the vale with the message, Cecile has surrendered time for eternity. Cecile, French? Her accent was Cockney, her habits Anglo, her dress foreign. And now dead?

Cockatoo is silent. Cockatoo knows not what to say. Cockatoo sits motionless on his perch behind the bars of his cage, unable to speak, unable to move, unable to voice his distress.

What was she telling you with her stick banging against the floor of your mind? You ran down the stairs with a wind at your back, a long staircase with a flight leading only downwards. Who could go upwards? And as you ran down were you aware of another flight leading from the old lady's room to the top of the house? There were more stories than the one to which you sat patiently listening.

But French? You are astonished. An appeal to the window, to open the curtains, admit the light, allow her to see more clearly up the long street, to see, people walking, into shops, out with bags, into doorways, carrying parcels, dodging puddles, poking umbrellas to the clouds, flapping scarves, beating down the flags in the searing sun of summer.

The street sees all seasons, the street with houses on both sides. The traffic of life, inseminated in private, born and presented to the public face, the street busy with cars, bicycles, bus stops, lorries, vans, delivering, using this direct line on which you stand and all of them, all of them, all of them, machines. There is no time, there is no light, there is no space. People have no substance, trees are statues, the sky is a sheet of paper which someone has coloured for the benefit of daytime. Cecile is dead.

You For Christ's sake, you bloody bird, say something! Waggle your beak!

 People!

But you see them all as they tighten their grips on their carrier bags. Hold on to the goods, let not that go which cannot be taken beyond the stone! They know that the hole in the earth admits only of bodies and they cover it up with a stone. A miserly stone.

Call that a story! Cecile, you never finished! You were listening and she thought you weren't interested.

You sit heavily on the kerbside, lost to the world, your feet dangling in the gutter.

Sweeper Excuse me, duck.

He shoulders his heavy broom behind a pile of yesterday's filth.

 Trip you up, I will.

He smells. He smells of all that you would rather not know, of the dirt, of the black hole in the earth, of the chippings of stone, carved from the face which will be the remnants of her story, a story which needed a strong stick to emphasise the points which nobody heard, accusations, deceits, fantasies, which you wanted to hear. You listened. You were captivated. He smells of the droppings.

He leans in his boots and stares at you. You have stopped him in his track, the gutter. Like Cockatoo, he is silent. Like Cockatoo, he watches you, waiting for a happening, leaning on a cracked column.

Melinda holds your arm to raise you to the pavement and the sweeper continues down the gutter, solemnly pushing his pile, occasionally collecting an extra burden.

You　　　　Fornicate!

Melinda　　What, now? Here?

You　　　　It's the only way. Keep life going, got to keep on at it, mustn't let the side down, not let death have the last word.

Melinda　　But, not on the pavement.

You　　　　Anywhere, doesn't matter.

Melinda　　Is it really that urgent?

You　　　　Life and death.

She feels her skirt, giggles, looks at people, wonders fleetingly whether they would notice, knows the answer but all the same considers the hardness, the coldness, the unusualness of doing it right then and there in the open street. Dogs do it. And get chased for it.

Melinda　　I'm not an animal.

Chapter 10
DAKS

The square, Chelsea, a coffee shop
Daks, a Taxi Driver, a Gentleman, a Barista

Bill Daks feels he might have made a wrong choice, though he has no doubt about his powers of deduction. He also is fully aware that the zoo where the incident occurred and the area known as Chelsea where he has established the offensive weapon was bought, are on opposite sides of the city; and that being an indisputable fact, verified by several well-respected maps and street guides, he will need to ascertain the time taken to move between the two locations, and whether the movement may be motorised, public or not, or pedestrian. He is undecided as to which would be the better place to start, given that he is currently midway between the two. His knowledge of the city is, unfortunately, not as good as that of some taxi drivers, upon which fact he reflects with some regret. Maybe he should have paid more attention to the geography teacher.

Daks   Right. The bird pointed that way. But I can't fly so how? Do I take the Tube or find where I've left my car? There's an Underground station over there and I think my car must be off on one of the roads leading away from the square. Can't have parked it on the square itself. Actually, not sure I parked the car at all.

He hails a taxi.

Driver   Where to, mate?

Daks   You can take me to Triumph Street.

Driver   Where? Are you sure? I never heard of no
          Triumph Street. Do you know where it is?

Daks points.

Driver   Very helpful. OK. You're the guvnor.

He drives off into the stream of traffic. Daks watches the
taximeter.

Daks   Scandalous. A fiver!

Driver   Nearly there, Sir. Just turn down here. Whoops.
          No, wrong way.

The taximeter records a tenner.

Driver   This is it, Sir. Which side are you wanting?

It is a street of terraced houses, two storey, not the style
Daks was expecting.

Daks   Is this Triumph Street?

Driver   Sir.

Daks   Chelsea?

Driver   Oh, Chelsea. Now, if you'd said that in the first
          place, I could've got you here a lot quicker. As
          it is, Sir, I'm not too sure myself. But I've got
          the knowledge. So let me re-assure you – this
          is the place you asked for.

Daks emerges from the cab. He looks around. No sign of
a bakery, not even any kind of shop. He passes a ten-
pound note through the open window.

Daks   Keep the change.

Driver   It's 60p more, Sir.

Daks has walked off. The taxi driver considers getting out
of his cab to pursue his fare. He hoots but the bloke must
be deaf or something. He doesn't even make a hint of
turning round. He hoots again. Nothing. He hoots a third
time. Still nothing. He drives off.

Daks is looking at every door. They are all painted in drab colours. Number 42. Number 44. Number 48.

Daks   What's happened to Number 46?

He crosses to the other side. Still the same drab colours. Number 51. Number 49. Number 43.

Daks   What's going on? Number 47 and 45 missing. Some weird street. Not a shop among them.

He walks the length of the street to the junction. He doesn't trust the numbers, but he is nevertheless concerned to check he's in the right place. Lace curtains in the windows. One has a model ship behind the glass.

Daks   Should be a street sign. Yes, there, just the one, high up. 'Triumph St'. I knew I was right.

He turns and looks back down the street. The taxi has gone. The street is empty. No cars, not a bike. No people other than himself, walking. Not even a cat, and it's not raining. He walks along the street again. Stops. He faces the door of a house that looks more or less like all the others but he decides it has a sign of promise so he rings the bell. The door opens to reveal an elderly gentleman.

Daks   Good morning, I am DI Daks of the Metropolitan Police.

He waves his card.

Daks   I'd like to ask you some questions about a potential murder case I'm investigating.

Old man   Oh, dear, that sounds a bit serious.

Daks   I'm looking for a bakery in this street.

Old man   Well, well, did you have some kind of sixth sense? There used to be a Mrs Tukes who lived here and she had a bakery at the back.

Daks   You say she used to live here?

Old man	Oh yes, many years ago. I was a boy at the time. We used to knock on her door and ask if she'd got anything nice. I remember the buns she made.
Daks	Buns? Did you say buns?
Old man	Yes, they were a sort of Chelsea bun, all curled up and full of currants. Penny for two. Ha'pence each, but of course that don't mean anything to you now with all this decimals and things. Not proper money it isn't and the prices, can't believe it how much they charge now just to get a bite to eat.
Daks	Excuse me. What did you say your name was?
Old man	I didn't, you never asked.
Daks	Then I'm asking you now.
Old man	Charlie.
Daks	Is that your first name or your surname?
Old man	It's what everyone round here calls me. It's not my real name but it's what they like to call me, so now it is my name.
Daks	And what is your real name?
Old man	I just said, didn't I? Charlie.
Daks	All right Mr Charlie.

Charlie grins.

Daks	I'm not concerned about your name, real or otherwise.
Old man	Oh, pity.
Daks	Because my main interest is this Mrs Tuke.
Old man	Tukes. With a S. Not plural though. Just one of her. Singular. You know. But it wasn't her name. No, not her first name. She married you

know. Mr Tukes. Not very good with your grammar, Sir.

Daks   Tukes, then, who you say lived here and ran a bakery. My luck is in. I've found a significant piece of the puzzle. Now then, Mr Charlie, I need to ask just a couple more questions. This is Triumph Street and what's the number of this property please?

Old man   Triumph Street! Cor, where d'you get that from? Hasn't been Triumph Street ever since God knows when. And I'm really sorry to disappoint you, this house hasn't got a number.

Daks   Hasn't got a number? What sort of place is this?

Old man   It's a respectable house, that's what it is.

Charlie shuts the door, leaving DI Daks sure that he's found the source of the murder weapon, sure of his astonishing powers of deduction, sure of his unlimited powers of interrogation. He retraces his steps to the corner of the street. The sign 'Triumph St' is certainly there on the wall of the house. It is a dark blue sign, with white lettering, typical of the style which was disused half a century ago, but Mr Daks is unaware of this fact. He checks lower down the wall but there's only the one sign. He turns around to make sure he hasn't missed anything. Nothing.

Still certain of his rationality he banishes all hints of doubt arising in his mind. Except that he doesn't actually know where he is, he doesn't completely know how he got here and he has no idea of how he is going to leave. All this time there has been only himself in the street and that old fellow at the door, now closed. He decides to go back to Mr Charlie.

A lace curtain twitches. He stops, not certain if this is Charlie's house, they all look so similar. The lace curtain falls gently to rest. Daks considers for a while then rings the bell again but there is no answer. He is left standing on the pavement studying the colour of the front door. Then, to his amazement he notices a faded painted sign on the stone lintel: 'Elizabeth Tukes'.

Daks   So this is the right house. I am in the right street and I have uncovered the source of the miscreant's item, your offensive weapon.

He chortles and walks gaily to the far end of the road. What he does not see at first is that above each doorway on the stone lintel there is a similar sign of faded paintwork. 'Reginald Tukes', 'Mary Ann Tukes', 'Joseph Tukes & Son', 'Albert Tukes', 'Josephine Tukes', 'George Tukes', 'Thomas Tukes'.

Daks   Damn! The whole bloody street of them. All Tukes. And I'll bet he's one, too. Charles Tukes. The liar. Charlie indeed. Made me look one and all! Damnation take the lot of them.

He turns the corner and discovers he is in a lively thoroughfare; people, prams, cars, taxis, delivery vans, buses. The familiar scene of red double deckers is reassuring and he remembers his need for some refreshment.

A few yards on, he opens the door to a coffee bar. It's dark. There are old wooden tables and a motley collection of chairs, worn leather sofas into which you sink. People doing crosswords, working on laptops, talking into their phones while their friend stares into the distance, watching nothing, growing impatient. There's a hiss of steam, a scent of chocolate, fancy cakes at exorbitant prices. Hushed conversations. A laugh which is much too loud and obviously false. He looks around. There's an empty table at the back. Will the guy in front take it? He's ordering a takeaway. A woman with a baby pushes in front of him. Her pram knocks into his knee. All she wants is sugar.

Barista   It's on the table, madam.
            Sir?

Daks   Coffee please.

Barista   Yes, sir. What would you like?

Daks looks at the bewildering array on the chalk board behind the counter. Why do people have to be so rude? What happened to civility? It's not my day, is it? What the hell is this? Cardboard mugs. A stick of wood.

Daks   Just coffee, please.

Barista   And is that to be large or medium, sir?

Daks   Ordinary.

Barista   Large cappuccino. With chocolate, sir?

Daks   What? No.

Barista   Very good sir. Anything else, sir?

Daks   Oh, why not? I'll have one of those, please.

Barista   Chelsea bun? No problem, fresh baked this morning. You'll enjoy it.

Cockatoo weeps.

Chapter 11
MUSIC

The street again, another bakery
You, Cockatoo, Nelson, Melinda, another Shop
Assistant, a Barrel Organ Player

It's clear you have a problem with your consciousness. You like to think that what you see is what exists. But too often you see what you want to see and conversely, no perversely, you don't always see what you do want to see. And your identity. It's a pressing question. "Who am I?" You'd like a simple answer. But perhaps there isn't an answer, none at all, or not one that is acceptable or makes you feel comfortable or happy, not even cheerful. You have to muddle on as best you can. And perhaps a corollary. "Who is God?" And this regardless of whether you believe in God. Maybe someone invented God, maybe God does exist but without a capital g. Maybe God is a figment of someone's imagination, a desire to make sense of the world, a fervent wish to make it mean at least something, that it's not just a tale told by an idiot, full of sound and fury, signifying nothing. Although that probably is what it is. So poor old Moses gets an utterly unsatisfactory reply when he dares to question the appearance in, or is it of, the burning bush. I am what I am. I am what I will be. You cannot even translate the enigmatic Hebrew phrase into your own tongue. You so desperately want the world to have meaning, purpose, value, that when you see an effect you very much want it to have come from a cause. But perhaps there is no meaning. Time passes. Space moves. Both of these happen, whether you want them to or not.

Pity poor Inspector Daks. But then stand back and turn the question on its head, your head, and instead of pity say to him "You idiot!" And even that may not be adequate because you are the idiot. Yes, you, the one standing proudly, the one who knows, the one who thinks everything you think is valid and true. "You idiot!" Don't even turn the question on its head, turn yourself over and stand on your head. Does the world look any different? Yes, of course, it's upside down. How amazing. And does it make sense? No more nor less than when it was the right way up.

OK, go ahead, call me a cynic. I don't mind. Here's the rub. You know as well as I do that Daks' powers of deduction are nothing like as fantastic as he'd like them to be. No, sorry, that is what they are, fantastic, something in his dreams, not reality. Oh dear! Here you go again, making statements about something you'd like to call reality, not having the faintest idea whether there is such a thing. It is what it is. It will be what it will be. Here now, not before, gone already. Did he, Daks, not exclaim Triumph? Did he not then make a leap into the unknown and prove to himself that he could go to Triumph Street. And ask the taxi driver to take him there, even though he'd never heard of it for all his knowledge. More odd still, Triumph Street is apparently where the taxi driver took him. Daks saw the street sign but was it there? Or did he only see it? And if he did see it, perhaps it was from long ago, a memory that reappeared magically in Daks' head. Just like the buns in Charlie's childhood bakery. Were they or weren't they? And was the café, where Daks ate a Chelsea bun, the real source?

You   Too many questions. You've tired me out.

But there are more questions. This whole confabulation depends on whether or not you killed Cockatoo. If Cockatoo is real, of course.

Cockatoo   Not real?

But, and you may well protest with vigour, the proof is that Cockatoo never did die, merely feigned death before rising majestically to his lofty perch.

Cockatoo   Lofty!! Oh, say that again, I like it. Majestic! Lofty!

Nelson   Bighead!

So, you have every right to protest your innocence, but unfortunately for you, your innocence or guilt is not actually in question. Daks has stated that you are (guilty, that is) and what the good inspector states is, ipso facto, true. Notwithstanding his clearly deficient skills in identification of a street, a house, a person within the said house, existence of manufacture of an edible substance, whether edible is correct, or actually inert, solid, hard, ability to recall said house, ability to notice facts material to the case, the list goes on. Moreover, Mr Daks does not question his knowledge of the conditions of life or death, or should that read life and death? Makes more sense like that. We live and then we die. Or do we die and then live? Is the bun that you partially ate… Wait! Did you only eat half the bun because you were already well aware of its dangerous qualities? Of its potential to cause grievous bodily harm? Can you do that to a bird?

Cockatoo   Why not? He is guilty, isn't he?

Nelson   Shut up!

To continue, or rather to go back a few steps to the defining issue at hand which is this awesome question that doesn't seem to go away: "Who am I?" Monsieur Descartes got it wrong. He assumed that his being alive depended upon his capacity to think. And writing in Latin doesn't excuse him. It is more likely that all life forms involve consciousness, an awareness of being. So we make the mistake, primo, that we can think while nothing else can.

Cockatoo **Told you!**

Nelson **Shut up!**

Secondo, we make the next mistake assuming that it is being conscious that makes us alive. It is a dreadful convoluted puzzle that doesn't get any easier with trying to tease out the answer. So, you have a choice, continue trying to get the answer, which you know will be utterly fruitless, or forget all about it and just do what you have to do. And please don't turn this around by asking how you would know what you have to do. That is pointless, you have to do it so just get on with it and stop dilly dallying on the doorstep. Melinda is waiting for you to make a move.

You **Phew!**

Melinda **Have you finished cogitating then?**

You **Yes, we'll go down here.**

Melinda **Good.**

You join Melinda and, holding hands, walk off happily into the sunset, which isn't due for several hours. You hear music though you can't see where it's coming from. It's a jolly sort of tune, waltz-like. And you can't work out if it's someone playing a recording or what sort of instrument it is. You pass a bakery.

Melinda **Shall we go in here?**

You enter the shop. The bread looks fresh. It might even be handmade. Under the counter is a display of pastries, very fattening, delicious, lots of cream, marzipan, cherries, chocolate, a strawberry tart, gleaming red.

Melinda   Do you sell Chelsea buns, please?

Assistant   Oh, I'm sorry Ma'am, we don't.

Melinda   Do you happen to know where we could buy some, then?

Assistant   A supermarket, perhaps. They often sell that sort of thing. It lasts longer so they don't have to worry about the shelf life.

You go back out into the street. The music is still audible, the same tune. You wonder if the musician doesn't get bored. Then you see him, he's playing a barrel-organ. You tell Melinda you're confident you haven't been in a supermarket today. She nods but seems to be more interested in the music. You say you're sure it wasn't here that you bought the bun, but that, on the other hand, you don't actually remember where it was. Melinda has stopped by the barrel-organ player. You ask her if it would help if you got a map of the city and drew, say, a circle around the zoo so you could, say, work out a likely radius in which to search. You say likely because you're fairly certain that you walked to the zoo this morning but, of course, it's now such an ingrained habit, you could have got on a bus. Melinda is fascinated by the barrel-organ. You say to her how you like puzzles. She is touching the handle.

Melinda   Can I turn it, please?

Player   Of course.

The music is the same, but its rhythm is rather uneven and too slow. She giggles. The barrel-organ player smiles. He beams out at the passers-by, quite unconcerned. He takes the handle back from her.

Melinda   Do you collect money?

She looks on the pavement, sees no hat or bowl or other collecting receptacle, nevertheless, takes her purse out from her shoulder bag, opens it.

Player   Why?

She has a coin in her hand, and is offering it, looking for somewhere to put it. You say you think it could be an idea to go back to the zoo first then try to retrace your steps.

Player   That's all right, love. I just enjoy playing.

Melinda   What's the piece called? It sounds so familiar.

Player   The music of life.

Melinda puts the coin to her lips.

Melinda   A kiss for you!

She giggles.

The player keeps turning the handle, releasing the dance of life into the tumble of voices and traffic in the street. A cacophony of people who never stop talking as if their lives depended on their capacity to think, to make rational arguments, to argue without just cause, to ascertain effects, to establish themselves as sentient, sensible beings. They never miss a chance. They hardly hear the music jogging them. Do they notice the world pleading with tears running down her face, their own bodies screaming for peace, their cousins, the birds, the animals, the insects, all showing them how to simply be?

The player smiles. You haven't heard.

You   I think the zoo is that way. I'm not sure how far it is but I think we can walk. It's not raining.

Melinda is standing beside the barrel-organ, her hips swaying, her feet skipping in anticipation. The old man is unmoved. He turns the handle and the music pours out, note after note, bar after bar, waltzing into the horizon, and when the tune comes to an end it starts all over again as if there was nothing else in the world to do.

Melinda   What?

You   I said I thought we could go to the zoo.

Melinda   You just don't get it, do you?

You   What?

Melinda   The pleasure of just being and dancing to the music.

You   Oh that! It's OK. A bit repetitive.

Cockatoo smiles.

Do you remember when you were at school, dreaming. There would be the teacher, droning on and on. Talk about repetitive, they certainly had the knack. Absolutely bore you to death, they could, going on about getting it right, wouldn't let go until you did. Counting lessons, spelling lessons, the laws of physics lessons, the discovery of the globe lessons, history, Latin, French, poems by heart, on and on and on. Until you heard the birds singing high above and you called softly to them. "Come on down and play with me, please?" Stupid teacher, pretending to be cleverer than you. "I'll let you sit inside my desk." And you'd snuggle the little bird, smuggle him in and all the other boys would start to giggle. "Stop laughing!" Oh, rhapsody! Listening to the song of the little bird. And you'd imagine the walls of the silly classroom crumbling all around you and soon you would be free to roam out into the world. The windowpanes dissolving and turning back into a beautiful sandy beach. The blackboard chalk, squeak, squeak, screech, oh my ears, stiffening into the white cliffs of Dover, looking out to sea, defending our nation, the inky black inky ink losing its poison and flowing clear over the rills of the gravel and the desks themselves sprouting, growing, tall majestic oak trees commanding the bountiful earth to sing a song of joy to the heavens. Oh, little bird!

Bang! The teacher's cane misses your face by a fraction and still he goes on. One and one is two, two and two is four, four and four is eight. Your dream is shattered forever.

You I didn't kill you.

Melinda Why are you crying?

Melinda has seen the tears staining your cheeks.

Melinda I love this music.

Melinda beams her smile at the musician. He winks, just enough for her to see and turns the handle ever so slightly faster.

Melinda Come on, then let's carry on.

You stand.

You No.

Melinda What?

You I think there is something here with the music. It gets you, doesn't it?

Melinda Yes, and it belongs to him.

You move on together along the street delving deeper into the melée of people going about their business. The sound of music gets fainter until it is drowned forever in the traffic of human commerce. Only Cockatoo can hear it.

Chapter 12
JAMES
A police station, a different street, your flat
A Desk Sergeant, You, a homeless man, Melinda

You might well ask what happens next. For the life of you, and not for the first time, you find yourself in a situation without any idea of how you got to be there in the first place. You rack your brains but that just hurts.

You are standing at the reception desk of a police station, apparently on your own, for there is no sign of the blue serge jacket. Melinda is not beside you, and you are being questioned. You think you have entered the station of your own volition in order to ask where the zoo is, but it occurs even to you that such a simple request would not require such a measure. And now it seems, again not for the first time, you are about to be interrogated. The desk sergeant is kind enough, but he is also stern and not to be deflected from his duty.

You look around. It is very much like a police station. It has a smell of fear and the door beside the desk is protected by a keylock. And then you notice something that disturbs you, though why it should, you don't know. The sergeant at the desk is in uniform, his jacket is well fitting, done with shiny silver buttons, and he wears a tie, which you don't. He is asking you the obvious question, why you have bothered to disturb the peace of an establishment of law and order by assuming that you need an answer to such a simple request as to the location of a commonly found city utility, namely the zoo.

You I need to get there.

Sergeant   PC Jenkins! Take him away!

The constable takes you roughly by the shoulder, opens the door and deposits you on the pavement. You are a bit surprised because you thought you were going to be banged up for the rest of the day. Now you're thrown onto your own resources and you stand blinking in the brightness of the day, your ears assaulted by the traffic: babies in prams, police car sirens, ambulances, taxi drivers swearing, people shouting at no-one visible because they're talking on their smartphones to their friends, their children, their work colleagues. Melinda is nowhere to be seen. Nobody cares about you, nobody cares about anybody, everybody is busy minding his and her own business. A giant flickering illuminated advert is trying to convince you that you cannot live without whatever it is it is trying to sell you, a car, hair care, nail polish, a holiday in a tropical island, the chance of winning millions, your new dream house. Huge letters announce in gaudy gold, red and green, Baxters, Armstrongs, Rogers and Sons, CareView, SelfGrow, CostLittle, Poundless. You don't care. You don't care about the people around you. They're all strangers, who happen to be getting in your way, impeding your thoughts, preventing your easy progress. To where, you don't know, from where, you only have a slight recollection. Whatever did happen this morning? Is it true that you were in the zoo? Do you have to return to the zoo or would it be safer to go home, if you could work out the way to either of those places. Where the hell are you? Who are you? Oh, my God, here we go again. Not that impossible question. Think of Dinkins, Donkins, sorry, Johnkins. Cups of tea – in the morning? Have you completely lost track of time? You don't know where you are, you don't know when you are, you don't know who you are and all the while you are immobile in a teeming high street in the middle of a world class city which has shops, and zoos, and bakeries which might sell Chelsea buns and supermarkets which do sell Chelsea buns, and offices and police stations and bus stops, and streets which only exist in the imagination of Inspector Daks, youths who are rude to you and a Cockatoo who has flown from his perch on top of a statue on top of a column in the centre. Life is hell.

You   Where is Melinda?

You crouch down against a shop window. There's another guy on the pavement beside you. You exchange glances, then conversation. You ask his name.

James   James.

Silence.

The world is passing by without a care to notice either you or him. As if you don't exist at all, two pieces of detritus tossed aside by the stream as it tumbles over a rock. You don't think you're homeless, you don't think of yourself as down and out, you have dignity, your own personal sense of self-worth, small though it is. Deep down you do know who you are. It's only your thinking self that intrudes with pointless questions.

James   Relax.

You slide down to the pavement. It's cold and hard.

James   My wife died.

You listen. The traffic is unceasing. You are too distressed to move elsewhere.

James   I forgot my keys.

You try not to look at him, he's probably smelly and his hair is long and greasy. You wish now that you hadn't started talking to him, yet his voice is cultured, not even a regional accent, ordinary. In normal circumstances, he'd be well respected, a scion of the community. Either that or someone who has no problem being a swindler. Your imagination is excited. He could have been a stockbroker with pots of money, or maybe just a borough council bureaucrat. You keep your eyes away from him, staring at the grey asphalt in front of you. Spots of dried chewing gum. Smears of something you'd prefer not to know about. A scrap of newspaper. A discarded elastic band.

James   I was so upset, I just went out for a walk.

Feet, brown leather, black, trainers, sandals, high heels, plastic, shiny, grubby, polished, scuffed, silent, shuffling, clipping, one after the other, this is the way a journey is made, put one first, the other will follow, made up of a thousand steps, journey's end, the destination will take care of itself, enjoy the journey for its own sake, need to get there, away from here, how far, not long, get there soon, least said, conversation, he's still talking to you. Concentrate!

James   The door closed behind me.

He must be an idiot. Stop listening to him, get up and go. You have a self.

James   I walked for six hours.

He's going to tell you his story. Are you interested or simply too tired to do anything else? You do have purpose. You don't have to be sad, full of self-pity.

James   I was walking away and there was no-one to come and look for me.

He must have children. Or maybe not, perhaps they've all grown up, flown the nest. What point is being alive? You wish you knew. If you knew you wouldn't be stuck here on the pavement with all the traffic, people, mothers, lovers, shoppers, office workers, cleaners, salesmen, drivers, passengers, ticket touts.

Silence. Is he going to tell you more? The shadows of the buildings darken.

James   I don't know why I didn't ask for help.

Do you know? You could ask for help. Pride. Secrets. Shame. Guilt. Trying to be someone you aren't. Measuring your self against the aspirations of your teachers. Your betters. The ones who know. They have experience. They can tell you. Yet they didn't. You listened too much. Not too little. They flattered, cajoled, bullied, whipped, smiled, gave you detention, sent you to bed, eat up your greens, pudding later. Be good, be quiet, do this, do that. Commands, for the sake of commands.

James   The house is still there.

You   What's your other name?

James   Robinson.

Ordinary. Like you, really, nothing special. But you are, you know that. You have importance, because you are. People passing by. Traffic moving. Clouds. Everything in motion. That's life. Immobile dies. You must get answers. To which questions? Oh, hell!

You   I've got to go.

James   Sure.

You don't move. But you hear a voice calling. It sounds familiar though you can't quite place it. Then you see a police car has stopped at the side of the kerb and Melinda is beckoning to you from the window.

James   In trouble now.

You pretend not to hear. You get up and cross over to her.

Melinda   Get in.

You do as you're told. Sit in the passenger seat. Look at her, wondering, what on earth she's doing in a police car, not just in it, driving it. At least you know, now you think you know, what happened when she disappeared. When you were in the police station, she was there too, nobbling some keys to a car. You are amazed and then you are worried. Is she a policeman, policewoman? Is she the real one and the Daks character is a fake? Or maybe they're both in it together. How on earth did you get yourself into such a mess? What started off as a perfectly ordinary day. No! No such thing. If it's perfect it can't be ordinary, and vice versa, if it's ordinary it can't be perfect. Logical illogicality. Nice phrase. Anyway, what started off as a perfect day. Oh, stop it. You knew right at the start it wasn't going to be perfect. Did you? It could have been, perfect. But then how would you know what a perfect day would be? You'd have to wait until it had ended to find out if it was, had been, perfect, or just shitty as most days are, were. Oh God! For Heaven's sake, just let go of these stupid arguments. They don't lead anywhere. Maybe not, but they are fun. Fun! Is that what you call it? Well, it must have some attraction, or you wouldn't do it so much. Don't! Do! Shut up! Back to the beginning. The beginning? Well, got to start somewhere. Fair enough. Back to where you started then. Can I continue? Please do. All right, then, maybe it was only ever going to be an ordinary day. Ordinary? No, that doesn't work. It's not ordinary when you get into such an awful situation as this, sitting, in the passenger seat, in the front of a police car, with Melinda sitting beside you ready to drive off. Melinda! You even know her name. And she knows yours. She's been helping you. Maybe she's still helping you. Could be. She's looking at you.

Melinda   Hello!

You Is this your car?

Melinda Well, it doesn't physically belong to me.

Melinda drives off into the traffic. You look back at James on the pavement. Poor old guy. You could have helped him if you'd been a bit more sympathetic towards him and a bit less wrapped up in your own ego. You could have given him some money, helped him to get back to his house. It could have been mutual. You help him, he helps you.

You Where are we going?

The car is stopped behind a bus.

You Could we stop a mo, please?

You get out of the car and drag James to his feet. He's not quite as repulsive as you first thought. Either that or having sat next to him you've become accustomed. Or it's your own smell anyway. You bundle him into the back seat. He looks horribly bewildered. Melinda drives off. She says nothing as if what you've just done is the most natural thing in the world. And she seems to know where she's going because she simply checked to see if you've got your seat belt on, glanced at the back, and followed the traffic.

Melinda Is this right?

You nod. She turns the corner into the street where you live. To you as to her, this is the most natural thing in the world. No 41, your house, where you live. She leaves the car by the side of the road. It's a police car so nobody's going to question if it's meant to be there or not. It's a double yellow line. A bus route. It happens often enough.

Melinda Got your keys?

The three of you go up the steps. Into the hallway. You point up the stairs.

Third floor.

It's dull, without personality. Lino. Timed light switches. Brown paint. The sash windows on the landings need cleaning.

You open the door to your flat. Inside is as you left it. There's a lingering smell of coffee and your dirty cup is in the sink. There are grains of sugar on the table. And your dirty spoon. For some reason your bedroom light is still on. You switch it off and shut the door. You never make the bed. Or open the curtains.

You   The bathroom's that one.

It's the only door with frosted glass. James points to his ragged clothes but, even to him, what is happening now is so natural, it's what he'd expect. He's in need of a bit of a wash so he has one. The water in the bath is warm, the shampoo is pine scented and there's a clean towel on the rack. What has been a nightmare that seemed to occupy the whole universe has suddenly taken a break for normality, kindness and compassion.

You   I've put some clean things on the chair out here!

James looks a new man as he comes into the sitting room. Melinda has gone and you are waiting. You have been tidying up, trying to tidy up. You have put two books back where they belong. You have put some of the letters and papers into a pile, to be dealt with. Your old sweater is draped over one of the armchairs. You have straightened one of the pictures on the wall, though you have no idea how it could get so off-straight in the first place. You've made an attempt to clean the dust off the frame. You've opened the curtains and looked out onto the enclosed gardens below. Several plane trees tower above your third floor window and it seems nobody ever goes into the gardens because the railings are always locked and none of the residents is allowed to have a key, so you've been told. You're going to make some fresh coffee.

James   Is it OK if I sit here?

You   Do they fit? You're about the same size as me, I think.

James sits in the one unencumbered armchair. He looks quite presentable, though of course, he could do with a haircut and a beard trim. It's wonderful what cleanliness does for a person.

Silence.

You   I suppose you'd like something to eat?

He smiles.

You go into the kitchen and rummage in the cupboard. Maybe the fridge. Breadboard. You return to the sitting room with a cheese sandwich. James eats.

James   Have you got any beer?

You   Oh, sorry, I don't drink.

You sit watching him. He looks for a place to put the plate. You begin to be fascinated by him. He is urbane, well mannered. Only his long hair and his overgrown beard disguise the wrinkles on his face. You wonder how long he's been shut out from his home, living on the pavement, riding the buses to keep warm, hunting in bins for thrown away food. You were so close, it could have been you. You take the plate from him and put it on the table, on top of one of the newspapers you never finish reading.

Silence.

It is rather a waste, isn't it? You say you want to keep up with what's going on. You read a headline, start the story, get bored and skip to the next headline, turning the pages looking for something of value, of interest, to perk up your nostrils, to give you a thrill, but the sensationalism is never worth the effort, it's only ever meant to satisfy morbidity, a story fabricated from half-truths, elaborated from a supposition into a detail that bears no relation to what did happen or sometimes what might happen. And slowly you sink into the torpor of asking yourself questions that have no answers, questions that only torment you, questions that you turn over and over in your head until it hurts so much you want to spit them out but have nowhere to puke them.

James   I used to run my own business.

His voice brings you back and you sit up to take notice of your guest.

I was trained as an economist and I...

You smile.

It wasn't easy at first but when I started to get a list of clients who respected me, and more importantly, paid me, I began to enjoy it. I was helping them with their business plans. They call it consultancy these days, but I never thought of it that way. I wasn't pushy but I knew I had a skill to offer.

You think of your skill.

We had a good life together. I had an office. Mary did her thing. She was a florist. She used to create these wonderful displays for weddings and...

Tears come to his eyes. You look around for a box of Kleenex.

It's all right. I always get a bit weepy. She was much too young, you know. Barely 60.

He weeps again. Silence.

You   How did she die?

James   She cut her hand on some thorns. At least that's what the hospital said. They weren't roses, something else. The graze got inflamed and within two days she had septicaemia. There was nothing they could do.

You shake your head.

James   I was so distraught.

Silence. You want to know more. You want to ask how old she was. You want to probe. You want to ask what happened to his children. There is so much to learn about this man. Whatever made you stop Melinda so that you could go and invite him into your life? So often it is the people on first meeting you draw back from, you despise and hate, though you know nothing about them, except you see some disgusting behaviour, some way they have, irritating, bloody annoying, that puts you off for life, never wanting to be near them and yet there they are, they don't go away, and they're in your face, sitting next to you, sighing, spoiling your pleasure, interrupting your concentration, stuck in the middle of your field of vision. It is like a struggle with an angel you meet on a bridge from hell to paradise. How often are you going to have to learn this lesson? How many times before you accept its inevitability? You long to meet your shadow and every time your shadow draws near, you draw back. You have such a deep desire to be whole and yet when the opportunity passes in front of your eyes you look the other way. Not for me, someone else. Hey ho, pass on by. Another time maybe. I'm busy. Oh, the irony of the

Spirit. The grit of the angel, messenger of God. Such determination. He won't let you get away with it. He'll force you into the wrestling match, he'll hold you, twist you, break your thigh. He'll leave you gasping, pleading, crying out for help. You'll call to God, you'll shout for a passer-by, you'll yell in pain, surely someone must come. Of course, someone must come, of course God will help, of course you're not unnoticed, of course, of course. He's there, isn't he? He's already with you and you've taken it into your head it must be someone else, the kindly one, the compassionate one, the loving one, the one who wishes the best for you, who cares, who knows. You fool. You idiot. This is the one. This is the kindness shown, the care, the love. He asks and you don't reply. He comes close, you turn away. He grabs you, you shake him off. He stinks, he's ugly, he doesn't look appealing. He itches, he scratches, he shuffles, snuffling, spitting, moaning. And then his hold becomes a grip so hard you are forced into reality. And time there's no turning off, no dallying on a primrose path. This time it's for your own good, you know that. In your heart of hearts, you know, despite your protestations, despite your resistance, despite your strength, he is going to win. He is going to lead you into a new world, a field of green grass, where the troll is vanquished in the chasm below the bridge.

You   Don't you have children?

He weeps. The pain is so strong.

James   Susan is somewhere in Australia. Adelaide. She did use to call me.

Families are scattered across the globe. Cousins, uncles, offspring, grandchildren, drawn as humankind has always been to new horizons, green fields and opportunities that beckon from afar. How do we come to be in the places that we find ourselves? Was there some kind of fate that decreed you will be here or there? Or is it always chance? Why are you here now, with this man? Where is Melinda? You miss her. And that Daks? What is he up to?

You   Is she the only one?

James   No.

You think of your own family. Arizona. San Salvador. Hebrides. Is there nowhere sacred? Or is everywhere just ordinary? The view from your window seeps through the leaves of the plane trees. Would it be better if you could gaze across the Grand Canyon or on a mighty waterfall in Iceland? Maybe, you'd like to revel in an African jungle or skate across the vast tundra in Siberia.

James   Simon is in Newcastle.

You think of grime. Impenetrable accent. How ignorant you are with your limited travels.

James   He deserted me when his mother died. I say
            he's in Newcastle but that was years ago. He
            might have moved since then.

You remember, it's more than a decade since you spoke with your brother. Such a stupid spat and you swore then you'd never ever talk to him again. And the oath stuck, in your gullet, in your heart, in your veins, in your twisted mind. And now, try as you might, you can't lift the receiver to call him, or send him an email to say… what? That you forgive him? Well, it sure wasn't your fault. It never is. So it has to be him. And he won't say sorry, not in a million years will he say that. Utterly beneath him, his pride, his dignity, to have been so offended, how could you, how could you? Money. The grubby little tyke. Always grasping more, always demanding that you give him his due, his fair share, never satisfied with what he's got, the bastard.

You   Such a pity.

You hypocrite!

Cockatoo crows.

Chapter 13
KEYS

The police station
Daks, a Constable

Inspector Daks has returned to his office. He's finished writing his notes about his attempt to find the bakery, though he wasn't sure whether the guy was called Jukes or Tukes, something like that, but not very important because as it turned out he wasn't the baker. So no harm done. On the way back to the office he's bought a bagful of Chelsea buns. He's taken quite a liking to them. But he's utterly fed up with coffee in cardboard cups. Disgusting, tasteless.

There's a knock at his door. A constable in his shirt sleeves.

Constable   Have you seen the keys to my Escort?

Daks looks up briefly shrugging his shoulders.

Constable   They're not on the rack.

Daks is not interested. His officers are always losing something, the careless blighters. If it's not car keys, it's a file, their wallet. Just hope they don't lose their warrant card.

Daks   Have you looked in your own pockets?

The constable goes out. He sits at his desk, scanning his computer screen. The phone rings. He answers the phone, gets up, puts his pen on the desk, picks it up again, straightens his trousers, decides not to put his jacket on, puts his pen back on the desk, puts his jacket on, buttons it, smooths his hair, looks at the screen, picks up his pen

127

for the second time, goes downstairs. He opens the door to the front desk.

Daks gets up to shut the door. Wretched staff. He sits back in his leather chair, takes another bun from the bag, dunks it in the lukewarm coffee, wipes the drip from his chin, puts his feet on the desk.

The constable greets the sergeant. There's a woman waiting at the desk. She looks on patiently while the two officers exchange banter. She's holding a bunch of keys in her hand. The desk sergeant motions to the constable that the lady has asked to see him, in person. Nudge. The constable is surprised and even more surprised when he recognises the keys. He's delighted, of course, and he looks up to see the woman disappearing through the front door.

Cockatoo laughs.

Chapter 14
A LETTER
Melinda's place
Melinda

He doesn't seem to want know about me. I'm not sure he even knows where I live. Not the best place in the world. But it'll do for getting to work. Up on the train. Home.

Take my jacket off. Coffee. My blouse. Uniforms. Oh god, that's better. Relief. Let them be free. Hate that feeling of being tied up. Skirt.

Piece of toast. Marmalade. Oh, mouldy. How long has it been in the cupboard. Must have missed it. Never mind. Silly sell by dates. Or whatever. Something else. New jar. My, this lid's tight. Pop. Butter in the fridge. Hard. Like winter. Nice day today.

My slippers. Pom poms. Why am I just flopping at this table? Oh, come on, sofa's more comfy. Put the telly on. Not that there's ever anything worth seeing. Adverts. People thinking they're funny. Actors arguing. She's got a lot of make-up on. Red lips, red cheeks. Can't be bothered myself. You either like me as I am or. Nice to make a change, though. When I go out. Put my arm in his. Hold hands. Warm. I like to be held. His arm around me. Like a big safety net. With his smile. His funny tooth. I wonder if he's sensitive about it. Try him out one day. Not too soon. Don't want to put him off. Be on my own again. Be nice to live with someone.

Letter. I picked it up. I'm sure I did. Where did I leave it? Basildon. Mum. So old fashioned she is. Won't have a computer. What do I want one of those for, I don't know how to use it, I'd get all muddled up, I'll just write like I always did, and you could write to me sometimes, too. Where did I put it. Blue envelope. Dear Mum. Here it is. Sitting on it. Giggle. Put my feet up.

Darling Melly. I've grown up, Mum. I've left home. Oh, well, I suppose it is nice. I liked it when I was little. I wonder where she and Dad got the name from. Dear Mum. Oh, Dad. You are my angel, do you know that. That's what you used to say. I've got wings. I loved the way you used to hold me. On your knee, bouncing up and down. Made me giggle. You'll grow up to be famous, you mark my words, Melly. I wonder, would you be proud now. I haven't really made it through the ranks. Sergeant, though. I'm doing my best, Dad. I am. Do you remember that day we went to the seaside? I got so cross with you. It was my game. And then you said I could have a ride on a donkey. Only there wasn't one. Cheat. I wonder what happened to my primrose pink top. It was my favourite. It means honey, my name. Sweetie. I like that. It's me. Sweetie Angel. Giggle.

Oh, heavens, Mum. It's not true, surely. Poor Mike. Oh, Mum, that's horrible. Yes, I agree he'll get over it. In time. Why did I only make one piece of toast? Four pages, Mum. But you don't say how you are. Oh, yes, over the page. Never change, do you? Just Mum.

Better write something. Don't want her to worry. She writes so much. What is there for me to say. Emil. Yes. Do you think he will? This drawer needs a tidy. Pad in here, somewhere. Pen. Green, no. Blue, better. Black. Dearest Mum. Better say how sorry I am about Micky. He never writes to me though. Doesn't even phone. Poor boy. He's rolling in it. Wish I was. Cramped up here. Two rooms and he's got a bloody mansion. I don't like her, though. Stuck up. Micky's worth more than that. Still, his choice, I suppose. No, I don't like her. Oh, God, do you think I was like that to him. Little brother?

Dad's dead. He's dead, Mum. Why? Did you know? I saw him looking so awful. You must have seen it. Poor Dad. Much too young. Mum, please. Oh bother, now I need a hankie.

More toast. Ought to have something proper. You've got to look after yourself. I know. I do. Sometimes. What would Dad say if he saw me slumming. You do just what you want, Melly. You're a grown girl, now, Melly. You don't have to listen to me. I brought you up. And you'll be fine. I'm proud of you, my little girl, my angel. Don't joke. Little. Nice thighs. I hate it when they say cuddly. They have no idea.

Mind this butter doesn't drip. This volume is too loud. Stupid programme. Oops. Sticky fingers. Haven't used this old blue paper for ages. Basildon Bond. Mum. Basildon. We used to go all up and down the street on our bikes. All our friends. Till we argued. And Micky fell off. Ought to have a fountain pen really, if it's going to be proper. Never mind. Why don't kids play in the street anymore. We used to. And then argue. Get cross with each other. And then he'd start pummelling me with his little fists. I bet I hurt him more than he hurt me. They must have heard us all up and down the street. And you used to come running out. And then you'd tell Dad. It didn't mean anything. He didn't care. But he did come out to see what the fuss was about. And Micky would go off on his own. Leaving me. And then I had to run indoors. On my own. You rotter. Leave me for that cow. I know we used to fight but you were my brother. Micky.

Oh well, never mind him. He's gone his own way. I met this lovely guy, Mum. His name's Emil. Like my name only backwards. Nice that, isn't it. Well, sort of backwards. Never could do logic. Is that what it's called. Bit like arithmetic. I can't tell you too much because. Oh, you know. Confidential stuff. Got to keep Bill sweet. Mr Daks, Sir. But I do like him, Emil. Nice name, isn't it.

Well, I can tell you where. In the Zoo of all places. I think you'll like him too, Mum. He's got curly brown hair. Not as dark as mine. And I think we're the same age. Well, he's a bit older than me. He lives in Notting Hill. In a flat. Yes, of course, he's on his own. Like me. I'm on my own. Well, I suppose you are too now. Dear Mum. Life's not fair is it? Cruel. I promise I'll come over as soon as I can. Would next Tuesday be OK? I don't know why I'm asking. It always is OK.

I'm dying to tell you about him. He's such a gentle man. It was so funny when we met. I had to behave with Sir there, of course. Then he said he had to go into this place to see someone he used to know. Oh, Mum, of course Emil, not Daks. I waited for him for ages. It's a good job I'm patient. That's my virtue, Mum. I think you helped me there. Dad didn't. He was always off doing things. Couldn't sit still for more than five minutes. Do you remember when he brought me back that big teddy bear. It was nearly as big as me. Is it still in my room upstairs? I could bring it back with me on Tuesday. Or maybe you'd like to keep it. Remind you of happier times. When we all sat at the table for dinner. Do you still make your Shepherd's Pie? Cor, Mum, I wish I could do it like you. I follow the recipe you gave me, but it never turns out the way you do it. I bet you've got some secret ingredient you put in. Yes, I know what you're going to say. Love.

Well, I do it with love too but it's still not like yours. Do you think Emil will like it?

Making me hungry now. Need something savoury. Tomato soup. Can I eat a whole can? I could always reheat it. Or put it in something else. Wouldn't it be nice to share again? With Emil.

Oh dear, Mum. I've been having all these thoughts and I haven't written any of it down. You write such chatty letters. It's like living back when I was little. My life is so different now I've grown up. I wonder what you'll think of my hair. Please don't tell me off. It's so much easier. Emil hasn't said anything. Yes, I think we are in love. But he's a bit reticent, shy, you know. But there you are Mum, me, patient. I'll wait.

Oh bugger. The soup's boiling. I'm going to put a splash of yoghurt in. A bit of luxury. Ought to be sour cream I know but I haven't got any, so yoghurt. As long as it's not all blueberry flavour. Or rhubarb. Yikes, I'd hate that. Did that once in France, they put sugar in the tomato juice I ordered. Not the right taste at all. I suppose it is all a matter of taste. But my taste is how I like things. Could do with a Bloody Mary right now but I don't have vodka in the house. Could go down the pub after perhaps. But not on my own. Be seen as a slut. Wonder what happens if you put lemon in with this soup. Well, it'll stay wondering. When I'm with him we can go together. Sit and cuddle. And drink something slow.

God, what is this programme. Just trash. There must be something worth watching. Ooops, don't spill the soup. Oh, that's better. I've seen it before, but it'll bear another go. How do they come up with these stories? Nothing like real life. And you can't work out if you're meant to laugh. I like him, though. And the sparring between them is quite good. I'll finish the letter when this gets to the end. As long as I don't fall asleep on this sofa.

That was awful, that night. I woke up with such a stiff shoulder and I was freezing cold, too. Mustn't do that again. Though I bet I will. Got to get the 6:17 in the morning. I hate these early mornings. Get up, wash in a hurry. Scrape a coffee for breakfast. I'm going to change my job. Leave Bill with someone else to work with. He's all right though. Mr Daks. Sir. Ever so pedantic. And he always knows he's right. Which he isn't. At least, not all the time. He does have some good hunches but so do I and he never listens to mine. Well, maybe not never. There was that time we were chasing a thief and I said we were after the wrong guy. We doubled back and there he was, right under our noses. Brilliant. I like it when it works like that. Got a smile from the Super as well.

No, I'm going to change my job. What's this. Oh, that's ridiculous. It wouldn't happen like that for real. Makes a good story though. Yeah, go on. Do it.

Well, I could try lemon juice. It's quite nice with the yoghurt in. And I'll ask you to make me a shepherd's pie I can put in the freezer. Have to be in single portions. Not if I move in with Emil. Tea for two. Then it'll be three. And four. Grow up quickly. Make the most of it. It's an aspiration, isn't it. Something to look forward to. Big wedding. I'll even invite Micky and his. Miss Dad though, to give me away. Could ask Daks. God, what an awful thought. See him standing there all stiff. Heavens, no. Whatever put that in my mind. Perhaps because of Uncle Bill. I'll ask him.

I must put something on, I'm getting chilly. Put the heating on. My fluffy. Finish the letter. Hugs and kisses xxx. I will come. Next Tuesday. I'll just tell Daks I'm off for the day. He doesn't have to know why. He'll ask, of course. Important engagement. Then he'll ask if I'm ill or something. Nosey. Tell Micky I'm coming. You never know, he might turn up. The little sod.

These slippers are getting thin. I'm fed up wearing those sensible shoes. I wonder why we were in the Zoo. Daks can't stand wild animals. That poor bird. Cockatoo or something. Just fell down dead. Never seen that happen. Funny that, you hardly ever see dead birds. Where they go. In the bushes, the trees. Die alone. Everybody does. Get eaten by worms. What's that song. On Ilkla Moor Bahtat. Must mean something. To someone. Maybe everything means something. Arithmetic again. Funny language. Could put pom poms on our shoes. Be like Greek soldiers. What a laugh. But then we'd have to have something a bit more fancy for our uniforms. I could be a designer. To her majesty's service. We'd be the pompom police. Talk of the town. Laughed out more like. What a thought.

I'll do the washing up in the morning. Before I get the train. No. Better do it now. Have it hanging over me all night. I'm looking forward to seeing Emil again. He's got a cheeky smile. Like he's keeping something hidden. I like a man like that. Not secrets. But something to find out. Puzzle. I wonder if he's had a girl before. Must have. Be un-natural. I have. Not a girl stupid. Paul. Then Richard. OK, Mum, you don't have to remind me. And it wasn't me, it was him who went off with another. Glamour puss. He always did want me to put more make-up on. Why can't men be satisfied. I was sixteen with Paul. Fifteen. Our first kiss. And how he fumbled. It was in Victoria Park. Or was it Grosvenor. No, Victoria. Memories get mixed up. It was Richard in Grosvenor Gardens. No problem with his kissing. Or his fucking.

Lucky I never got pregnant. Dad would have been so angry. Do you think he knew? Yes, Melly, you can't keep secrets from your Dad. Just you try.

Oh, children. With Emil. But you're not to call me Melly. Not unless I give you permission. Which I will. And I'll call you Milly. Milly and Melly.

Must be time for bed. Mustn't forget to set the alarm. 6.17. Get another pot of marmalade. That bird. White feathers all spread on the concrete.

Milly. Giggle. Oh. You do love me, don't you? I love you. I do Emil, I do.

My jacket. Still on the chair. Did I switch the toaster off? Need more toothpaste.

Chapter 15
THE ZOO
In your flat, the police station, a taxi, the zoo, a café
You, the Desk Sergeant, a Keeper

You now have a conundrum. Not satisfied with the questions concerning the possible death of a cockatoo in the zoo versus the improbability that the assumed death was caused by a half-eaten piece of local confectionery, you now have to face the distinct possibility that Melinda, who you at first thought was just a nice woman trying to help you, then considered that, since she was driving a police car, she actually was a member of that illustrious force of peacekeepers but now are not so sure, given that she appears to have returned the car or at least its keys to the owner, Constable Trevor Jones, whereas Inspector William Daks, who must surely be a spoof, him having displayed remarkable ineptitude in probing a non-existent street, or perhaps a street that only appears when the necessity for its existence is paramount, is now to be seen, with his feet on his desk, consuming with relish a sample of the confectionery, in an inner office of the police station where you went to enquire about the location of the zoo, suggesting, if not proving, that he is a bona-fide officer, indeed an officer of higher rank.

Now this is a question worth answering. It is not like the questions which have plagued you, your identity, your shadow, your purpose in life, your interminable internal struggles. However, it is unlikely that this practical question will be any easier to solve. And you have forgotten the problem of where the bakery is, was.

As before, as on so many occasions, you have no idea where to begin. Of course, the best would be to ask Melinda herself directly, but that fruitful avenue is not currently available. You could ask James but that feels like an imposition. You could go out and follow your nose. You are sinking steadily into the realm of silly questions.

How did you know his name was Trevor Jones? Did he tell you? Were you there? Was he there when you were? How odd. Maybe he could help you, you never know, some of the most unlikely people are the ones who hold a key. Is that meant to be a joke, or did you just say that without thinking? Of course, he's holding a key, a very important one.

You get up to go and tell James that he's welcome to stay, but that you have to go out, just briefly, you'll be back in a jiffy, so not to worry, if he needs anything, just go hunting, you don't mind.

James isn't there. He's left a note. "Thanks for all. Got to go now. JR." This makes you cross. You went to a great deal of trouble to help him out of his predicament and this is how he repays you. You didn't have to bring him home with you, let him use your bathroom, give him some of your own clothes to wear. Hell, what's happened to those smelly rags he had? You'll bet they're just dumped where he took them off. You rush into the bathroom. Spotless. Bath clean. No sign of old clothes. Mirror wiped. Slightly damp towel hanging neatly on rack. Bathmat. Shampoo. You look outside. Chair. Tie hanging over the back. Didn't he want the tie, then? You never noticed. His beard. You're more furious than ever. You go to pick up the plate from the sitting room but it's not there. You go into the kitchen. Plate washed clean. On the draining board. Note. "Sorry, couldn't see where you keep the plates!" The bloody cheek of the man. Never in your life! What sort of guy have you let in to your life? Bloody hell! You could kick yourself. What a bloody idiot you've been. Melinda. Gone. This James. Vanished. Oh, Jesus! What are you going to do? What did he say his job was? Where the hell is Melinda? Just at this very moment you need her more than ever. Jesus!

You storm out of the flat, slamming the door behind you. Your keys are on the other side.

Cockatoo sniggers.

You stand mesmerised on the pavement then determine that you won't be fazed by what has just happened and stride with purpose to the corner, turn right and march up the hill.

Cockatoo is amazed.

For once, you take no notice of what Cockatoo thinks or does. His comments are too trite. You reach the main road, hesitate for a moment, turn left. You're fairly sure this was the way Melinda drove you all home. You pause for a moment to get your breath. It's not a long walk.

You walk into the police station.

You	I'd like to see Sergeant Jones, please.
Sergeant	Don't have Sergeant Jones.
You	Constable Jones?
Sergeant	Don't have him either.

You go back outside to the pavement. This is the right police station. You recognise the street, the advertising hoarding, the shopfronts. You go back inside.

You	Trevor somebody, then?
Sergeant	No Trevor here.

You're stuck. You know he was Trevor Jones. You know it was in this police station that you came to enquire about the zoo. You look carefully at the desk sergeant, but you don't really recognise him. Of course, there could be more than one duty officer on the front desk. Stands to reason. Couldn't have the same bloke all day and every day. You look at him. He looks at you.

You   Is there someone called Melinda who works here?

Sergeant Melinda?

You blush.

Sergeant Listen, Sir, when you came in this morning. No, yesterday morning. Whenever it was. You started asking stupid questions about where the zoo is. Now you're asking about your girlfriend, your boyfriend, your dad, your mum. What do you think we are here. All purpose marriage guidance? Agony Aunt? I suggest you leave us to do what we do and you go and do what you do. Is that fair? Do you understand, Sir? We do our job – you do yours, right? You leave us alone and we won't trouble you. Either that or I'll have you banged up. Goodbye, Sir!

It is the same sergeant, the same duty officer. How amazing that he remembers you and you don't recognise him. This sure is some strange upside down world that you inhabit. People who aren't what they seem. Places that don't exist. Birds who aren't dead. Statues that can see. People who have names which aren't their names. Tramps who are city financiers or whatever. Bakeries which vanish. Old ladies who die. No that is normal. Thank goodness some things are still true. But what about taxi drivers who claim never to have heard of a place in the city for which they have The Knowledge and then deliver you to the place you've asked for? What sort of world is this?

You're standing on the pavement, wondering where to go next. You hail a taxi.

You   The zoo, please.

The taxi drives off. You sit back in the leather seat and remember your cash is with your keys in the flat behind the locked door. It's why you walked to the police station. You lean forward to tap on the glass then think again. You'll wait. No, you mean you'll lie. Until you get to the zoo, then plead God knows what. You sit back. It's fine, you've got your wallet with your cards. No problem. You wipe your forehead with your sleeve. Oh, the streets of London. White Georgian terraces. Victorian yellow grimy brick. Houses, flats everywhere for mile after mile. Why do taxis always go through the back streets, never along main roads where there's something to look at?

The taxi drops you at the gate to the zoo. If only it could always be so easy. Then you wince at the cost of the fare and you know why it isn't. Luxury is a treat. At least you're not in James' shoes. And then the thought, horrific, flashes across your mind. Did James take your cash? Was that why you didn't notice it as you slammed out of the flat? You'll kill him.

The taxi has gone. You go up to the ticket office, peer through the little window, pay for the entrance, take the little grey ticket. How old fashioned. No 43792. They keep count. They might even remember you from last time. Quaint. You are about to ask for a direction but the little grey head has disappeared, so you push through the turnstile. How familiar. How déjà vu.

Yet you don't remember it at all. You don't remember buying a ticket. You don't remember anything except the time your head was being banged against the concrete floor and the cactus spines were digging into you. Ouch! You remember that all right. The bastard!

You Can you show me where the parrot house is please?

You walk through the asphalt jungle, wire cages, half dead tree trunks, noises, litter everywhere despite the proliferation of bins, ice cream cones, glass screens, smells, hay, scraps of food. An awful world, to be cooped up, imprisoned, no chance of flight, or a race across grasslands. How did humans ever think it was right to exert such command over other creatures? To catch them, drug them, fly them halfway across the world for other people to gawp at, to make children laugh, scared, bored. And then to claim it's for scientific purposes. You want to study them. What a cheek! It's what we do all the time. Do something awful and then invent a reason why it's OK. We really are half devil, half angel.

You go into the parrot house. Budgies, green tailed parrot, canary, gold macaw, pygmy parrot, green, red, blue, black, cockatiel, not quite, cockatoo. Empty.

You Can you tell me what's happened to the cockatoo, please? Why the cage is empty?

Keeper It died, Sir.

Empty. Vacant. No Cockatoo. You stand looking through the bars. There is nothing to see. The cage has been cleaned. Nothing. But, surely, the cockatoo isn't dead. You saw it, him, her, fly, talk, squawk, laugh, heard it mock, comment, judge. Wretched bird.

You wander disconsolately back to the main gate. You pass lions, elephants, penguins. You hear growls, shrieks, whistles, grunts. There are children, parents, nannies, au pairs. Keepers in green uniforms pushing barrows. Keepers smiling. Students joking. You pass them all by as if they didn't exist at all. They are simply obstacles, not worth a second or even a first glance.

You think of Melinda. If only she were beside you. You think of Inspector Daks and smile inwardly because he is not with you, thank goodness. But James Robinson, the scoundrel, running off like that. And Dick. And Cockatoo. Dear God, what in heaven is going on? You're sure his name was Trevor Jones so why on earth did the desk sergeant claim he didn't work there? You thank the taxi driver for being so kind, then curse him for charging you anyway. What a city!

You wander into the cafeteria. Formica tables and plastic chairs. A glass cabinet shielding worn out sandwiches and cakes from prying infant eyes and fingers. The lady is kind enough. She serves you a nondescript coffee which she calls a latte in a tall thick glass with a long spoon and two miniature biscuits. It spills into the saucer as you carry it to one of the vacant tables. You sit moodily looking out at the happy scene. Flowering shrubs, an acacia tree. Everybody except you uplifted, cheerful, on holiday, a day out.

You begin to laugh. Oh, the irony of it! You spent ages wondering how you were going to get back to this place. You were even stupid enough to try asking at a police station. And then you just get in a taxi who drops you at the main gate without any hesitation. Just money. That's all you needed. And not even real money, plastic. What a city! Now all you need is the bakery.

You   Bloody hell!

143

A lot of people turn round at your sharp ejaculation. People don't normally swear in a café. Not out loud. They stare at you waggling their little fingers. Tsk, tsk. They shake their heads. Tsk.

There in the glass cabinet – a plate of Chelsea buns. Full of Chelsea buns. Unmistakeable. There they are. Fresh from an oven. Not in a bakery. Here in the very place where you bought one before. Of course, so obvious. You'd buy one, take a few bites, jostle happily through the crowds. Put it back in the bag. You never did need to walk so far. It was there all the time. Idiot!

You   Sorry, everyone.

You walk out of the cafeteria. Then you rush back inside and buy one. Yes! The same taste. Bun found. Cockatoo lost. Melinda missing. Daks, James. Hell.

Cockatoo smirks.

Chapter 16
THE PARK
Regents Park near the Zoo
Melinda, Daks, James, Dick, You

Melinda is sitting on a bench in the park with a flock of sparrows at a respectable distance waiting for her to throw a few crumbs. She's eating a Chelsea bun and surely there must be some crumbs to scatter on the ground. Ever hopeful.

Melinda is waiting too. She keeps looking at her watch.

Daks   Sorry, I'm late.

Bill Daks. He sits beside her on the bench and immediately asks her the obvious question, why they are meeting here and not in the office. She says nothing but instead points to one of the other benches. James Robinson. Daks looks, not understanding the importance. He then points to another, younger man sprawled on the grass. Definitely younger.

Daks   I know him. At least I'm pretty sure I do. Don't know his name though but I've seen him in the last couple of days.

Melinda looks puzzled. She's never seen him at all. But she does know that something strange is going on. How did she, for instance, know to invite the Inspector to come to the park when at least one other character known to you would also be here? She looks at the Inspector.

Melinda   Where's your uniform?

Daks   I took it off.

Melinda   Incognito. Very wise. Do you want a bite?

145

Daks	No thanks, just had one of those in the office.
Melinda	Yes, they seem to be taking over the city. I see them everywhere.
Daks	I agree. I think that's part of the problem. We're looking for a specific place but we're getting confused by the similarities, if that's the right word, which it probably isn't. What I mean is... Look, I'd better tell you the truth. It's... Oh hang! Look, earlier I was sure I'd found the place, then it turned out I'd been badly let down. The wretched taxi driver assured me he'd taken me to the right place and then it turns out the place didn't actually exist at all. Now how that can happen, I haven't the faintest because I was there, of that I'm sure, I have no doubts. And then I turn the corner and, blow me, if there isn't one of these, ubiquitous, is that the word, ubiquitous, does that mean everywhere, anyway it's there, right in front of me. I go in and there's this huge pile of them under the counter. Very nice actually. I've been enjoying them. Feet up, you know, taking a bit of time to relax. Except for the younger members of my staff, keep coming in to interrupt me. They hardly knock and they're standing over me, demanding this, asking that, where's this, what do I do now, my God, have they got no nous. Now that's a good word, don't you agree? Nous! I like that. I'm not that bad, you know. Mind you, don't really know what it means, do you know? Gumption, too. Never mind, where were we? Actually, come to think of it, where are we? What are we doing

here? Park bench. Sunshine. Doesn't really count as work, does it?

Melinda isn't listening. She's looking intently at James Robinson. He is looking at her. He smiles.

Daks   But it makes a nice change. The open air. The bench could be softer, not like my chair. I quite like this. Could get used to it.

Melinda smiles.

Daks   Who is he?

Melinda   A bloke we picked up.

She throws the remains of the bun on the ground and instantly the sparrows are squabbling for the titbits.

Cockatoo watches but nothing untoward happens. The sparrows have pecked the ground clean. They look quizzically at Melinda and Daks, then leave to look for another benefactor.

Cockatoo is disappointed.

Melinda   He was down and out so we let him have a bath and a change of clothes. On the surface it's completely changed him, but I assume it hasn't really changed things for him. He's still homeless.

James is surrounded by the flock of sparrows. He is tearing Chelsea buns into pieces and scattering them for the birds. A few pigeons have joined the feast, but the sparrows are not put off.

He looks remarkably neat for someone who's homeless. His long hair is combed and neatly frames his smiling face. His beard is also long but it has been trimmed. He looks more like Jesus in western dress than a tramp or a beggar. He has the keys to your apartment in his pocket. Perhaps he would be more of a saint if he wore sandals

147

and a robe, but he is unconcerned. His mission today is to feed the birds. They squabble and peck, mob the pigeons, dart at crumbs, fly to a safe distance, return for more, their appetite undimmed and James has a substantial bag of buns to distribute. He has not a care in the world.

Dick, on the other hand, is lazing in the sunshine. He also has not a care in the world but that is not to do with his attitude to life, more to do with the fact that work has finished early and he's decided to enjoy himself. The tripod and theodolite lie beside him.

You wander disconsolately into the park. Once again you are sunk into the torpor of inaction, into the slough of interminable thoughts. So beset are you with your failings, your stupidity, your self-imposed imprisonment, that you fail to notice anyone. You walk within yards of the bench where Melinda and Daks are sitting. That the Inspector is in mufti is immaterial. You certainly don't see James or hear the excited chatter of the sparrows. And Dick is just another guy lying on the grass. The sky is as dark as it's ever been. Sunshine has no meaning. Warmth doesn't touch you. You walk not knowing in which direction you're moving, your shoulders hunched, the loss of your keys and your money racing one after the other around your brain, excluding any other thought or feeling or sensation. The grass might be soft or hard, the asphalt grey or green, there is nowhere to sit, to rest, nowhere that is forward, nowhere but the past from which you cannot escape. That this is a dilemma of morality has not occurred to you. You have made the prison bars that surround you and you are now, right now, building them ever stronger and higher, filling the space with filth.

Cockatoo is silent. Cockatoo inclines his head towards you. Cockatoo watches you with pity and disgust. Cockatoo is your friend if only you would hear his voice. Cockatoo never did die. It was all an act. Cockatoo is now contrite and would ask forgiveness but you have closed your space to anything, anyone, any creature who could give you absolution, help you, aid you, show you a way out of the dark wood of your rage.

You think of Mrs Johnkins, dead. What was she trying to tell you? And now you can't ask her. You should have paid attention. Poor Cecile.

Exhausted, you flop to the grass. Dick recognises you.

Dick   Hello, mate!

You look but all you see is another man lying on the grass. Nowhere to turn to. You want to be alone. You don't want this man interfering. You've got your own train of thought and you want to let it run. Even though you don't really want to. You're really fed up with the bickering, the repetition of endless worries. And as soon as you consider this it starts another train that won't stop. A circular track of words, words and more words that cannot be uncoupled, that buzz in your ear, block your nose and fill your mouth. A tangle of knots that no sooner do you cut one it grows and curls into another, even tighter, more convoluted than before. A gorgon's head of writhing serpents that one look will turn you into petrified immobility. You can feel nothing, not the grass, not the sun, not the warmth of this man offering you a tender hand with which to pull you out of your misery. He means well, does Dick. He's there to help. Your unconscious self chose this place to rest, chose it rightly for you to be lifted out of your despondency.

You look at him. He does look familiar.

Dick   You all right, mate? You look done in.

You say nothing. Why is he interested? You want to be private. He is looking at you.

You   I can't get into my flat.

Dick raises himself on his elbow.

You   And I haven't got any money.

Dick   Cor, bad luck.

Dick lies back on the grass gazing into the blue. You've said too much. You should have kept yourself to yourself. Not tell others about your troubles. Especially not some layabout who you've never met. Idiot. And yet. Why? Why not? He's inoffensive. He's even sympathetic. He's looking at you again.

Dick   You could go to the police.

What does he know? You're already in trouble. Every time you get involved with the police you get nowhere. No, worse than that, sometimes you get beaten to a pulp. No, not the police. They don't know how to help. Waste of time. Might as well just lie here till …

You jump. No! Not death. Not suicide. Not get tempted. It's a crime, a sin. Definitely not. Mustn't let yourself be driven to that point. Get up. Off the grass. Get out of this slouch.

Do something for heaven's sake. That's it, isn't it, heaven's sake. Not the devil, not Satan, not the tempter. Let heaven in for heaven's sake. That's it, isn't it. Get into a positive state. Now! Do it. Now! This moment, now.

You   What did you say?

Dick   What?

You   You said something.

Dick   I say lots of things.

You	Yes, but just now, you said something about what I should do.
Dick	I didn't think you were bothered. I thought you could go to the police.
You	Right!

You get straight onto your feet. You look down at Dick who is astonished at your sudden change. He's looking at you more intently than ever.

You	Dick! It's you.
Dick	Of course, it's me.
You	Jeez, I'm sorry. I was a bit lost just then. I thought you'd gone home. How come I didn't realise who you were?
Dick	I wondered why you were so strange. Go on, then. Go over there.
You	What?
Dick	There's a copper over there, on that bench there, behind you. I know he's a copper, cos I've seen him before. He thinks he's clever cos he isn't in uniform, but I can spot them, sniff them out. Easy when you know. My dad's a copper. He's told me all the tricks. How to get into a house. How to steal a car. How to show you're not afraid. Everything.
You	Oh, I'm not sure I want to get involved with the police.

You look where Dick is pointing.

More confusion. Sitting next to the man you definitely don't want to see is the girl you definitely do want to see.

You	Melinda!

Dick	No, not her. The bloke. He's in mufti but I can see he is a copper. He doesn't think I know but he knows me. He saw me when he came into the park. I know he did cos he gave me one of those looks. Nose, nose! Know what I mean?
You	Get him away.
Dick	Get who away?

Daks has heard you and Melinda has seen you. They get up and walk over to you and Dick. One has tight determined lips, the other a happy welcoming grin. One is delighted so is the other. Daks has pursued you and now he's got you right where he wants you. And Melinda has found you at last. Should you run? But in which direction? You look back at Dick who is still lying on the grass.

Then James gets up and also walks over to you. Five people is going to be a crowd with a lot of shouting and crying and laughing and then sure as sure there'll be a park ranger.

Cockatoo is excited. He is flapping his wings and screaming at the top of his voice. Such a commotion.

You hiss at Dick.

You	Get up!
Dick	What for? It's not me he wants to see. It's you who needs to ask him.
You	No, I want to see her, not him.
Dick	Well, they're both coming.

Which way do you go? To embrace Melinda while avoiding Daks. To smile at Daks and take Melinda's hand. To offer a branch of peaceful olive. To welcome both. To scorn the friendship, you desire so much and run away. And what the hell does James want? Where are you going to run to? You are clearly within the sights of four people all of whom you know and all of whom know you. You are no stranger except perhaps to yourself. This farrago of pain and pleasure may not be all of your making. You did or maybe you didn't purchase a Chelsea bun. You certainly ate one, or half of one. You didn't or maybe you did exterminate a white feathered bird in the zoo with a careless gesture. Or maybe it wasn't careless at all. Maybe it was deliberate. You fully intended to do harm. Or it was an accident. Or it never happened at all. What on earth was the purpose in going upstairs to listen to Mrs Dinkins' story, sorry, to Cecile Johnkins. Who on earth was she and what does she, did she, have to do with you. So many questions. So many answers required. By whom, by Daks, Melinda, Dick, James, all pressing down on you, bearing at you, approaching with menace and nowhere to run to. Open grass for miles around, not even a tree trunk to hide behind. A bench to sit on. Which bench, this one or that one. The road out of reach. You're petrified, caught in stone like a rabbit in the middle of the highway. Eyes blinking, frozen fear. You look up to the sky, to the hills. Which hills, those bumps in the distance. To heaven, surely there must be some salvation. You cry out, and no sound emerges from your lips. Only Cockatoo is gleeful with mirth.

Dick is lying on the grass. Melinda is smiling. Daks is grinning. James is ambling. Cockatoo laughs loud and clear.

James has dropped his bag of Chelsea buns and the sparrows have never had such a feast. Squabbling, chirping, flapping, twittering, greedily pecking, chunks, crumbs, currants, sugar, yum, yum, yum, yum, yum.

You   Hello, Melinda.

Melinda	Hello.
You	It's really nice to see you again.
Melinda	Me too.
You	I thought you'd gone.

You sigh. Then you glance at Inspector Daks. He has lost his fierce look. He seems to have softened. You smile at him.

Daks	You know each other?

Pretty unmistakably, the way you and Melinda are almost clasping each other. James, too, is surprised. But not Dick. Nothing surprises him. He's a man of the world. He isn't fazed by anything except not earning enough money. If only he had enough then he'd be fine. No worries. Just enough money. Fast car. Bird. Swank clothes. The biz. You can keep the champagne, but he'll have a bar with whisky, beer, lager, whatever. And a decent steak and chips. Something with a bit of heft. And bloody. Rare. Smashing. Nothing like it. A T-bone grilled to perfection. Cor. Wouldn't life be wonderful. Just enough money. Give up work, lie around. Go for a spin. Drive-in cinema. Bird on each side. One for odd days, one for even. Leather gloves. A spot of crime. Not get caught. Dad's a copper, remember. But not caviar. Can't stand the stuff. Tastes of seawater. Yuk!

Now, you, just listen to him. He's got plenty to teach you. Educate as you call it. But you're pathetic. You really are. Always getting into some tiswas. Claiming to know. And you know nothing. But you are the boss. He'll stay. Till he gets enough. What wouldn't he do with enough money? World's the limit. And you know he'll never have enough. Enough isn't finite. It doesn't ever come to an end. He'll have some, even a lot, millions, and it still won't be enough. So he'll always be wanting more. Enough won't happen. Poor Dick. Not ever.

You	I've lost my keys.
Melinda	What?
You	Well, not lost them, exactly. I shut the door and they were still inside.

James puts his hand in his pocket.

James	Here.
You	What?
James	You didn't lose them, or forget them. They weren't there when you left. I borrowed them.

You take the keys. They are yours, of that there's no doubt at all. So what on earth is going on? Why didn't you just ask Dick to let you in. He knows how to pick a lock. It would have been easy for him, but then, of course, you didn't actually know where he was. Well, you did, you thought he'd gone home. No fault, thank goodness. At least there's one avenue that you don't have to worry about. But how were you to know that the keys weren't there anyway. You don't remember not seeing them but then you didn't check your pocket before you slammed the door in your fury.

You	Thank you.

Daks moves forward.

Daks	What's going on? Taking keys without permission?

No harm done. Everything's going to be sorted. You've got your keys and best of all you've found Melinda. Hooray!

You	No, it's not a problem.
Daks	To you maybe. But it's illegal.

Oh no. He's going to start getting rough again. That didn't half hurt. I can still feel the spines digging into me.

You   Take it easy.

Daks   Don't you dare talk to me like that.

You   Melinda, let's go and sit down somewhere.

Daks   Not so fast. There's still questions to answer.

Cockatoo wilts.

Daks   You first. Name?

James   Robinson.

Daks   You need a haircut.

James smiles.

James   My wife died.

Daks   What the hell has that got to do with it? Address?

You look at Melinda, James, Dick.

Daks   Come on. Your address?

You   He hasn't got one. He's homeless.

Daks   Ridiculous. Do you ever tell the truth? A bloke like that. Smart clothes. Clean. Homeless. Don't give me rot.

Melinda   No, I think Emil's right. He is homeless. At least he was.

Daks   Emil! First name! What the hell is going on? What have you got that you haven't told me?

Dick sniggers.

Daks   You! Shut up!

You look at Dick. You look at James. You look at Melinda.

Daks   You! I've just about had enough of you.

Melinda	Sir.
	Sir, if I could …
Daks	No, you couldn't. I don't know what's going on. You're involved in it. So's he. And so's he. Not sure about that one. If he is, he'll see the sharp side of my boot. As for you! I'm going to get to the bottom of this. Once and for all. You think you can get away with murder. Picking up homeless guys. Swapping keys. Buns! That's what it's all about isn't it? You don't fool me. Bloody buns!

Cockatoo hovers overhead.

Daks	Get that damned bird back where it belongs!

The statue is watching with acute interest. His back is turned but he has eyes. Cecile is dead.

Daks	Right. You! Address?
James	I'm terribly sorry to disappoint you, officer. You see, my wife died and I …
Daks	Yes?
James	I sort of…
Daks	Come on. Address. For the third time I'm asking you where you live.
James	Well, I don't think it has an address. Not as such. It's a patch of pavement. It's where I live.
Daks	You're a vagrant. A bum. Tramp. Ne'er-do-well. Dressed in a smart suit you've obviously stolen.
You	Oh, officer. He didn't steal it. I gave it to him. I mean we did. We thought…
Melinda	It's true.
Daks	You, keep out of it.

Nothing is true. Nothing in this whole damn sorry tale is true. And I'm determined. I'm going to get to the bottom of it. You think you're clever. You all do. Especially him. Stop smirking.

I am Inspector Daks of the Metropolitan Force. You think you can get past me. You think that ganging up will stop me. Well, let me tell you, all of you, especially you, and you, you can't pull the wool over my eyes.

James You see, officer. Mr Daks. Nice name. Short. Yes.

The pavement. It's where I lie down sometimes. Now that my wife. You see. I'm free. Not obliged. But it's not an address. Not strictly. I sleep there.

I watch.

You are going to ask me about my work.

Yes?

You think work is what you do. What he does, she, and him there.

Yes?

I watch. It is my work. Watching. Seeing the world as it is. As it really is.

You see, officer, I invite you to look at him. Carefully, mind. Without prejudice. An open mind. He is the most faithful. Lying on the grass. I don't know his name, though he knows mine because you asked me. But I know him.

There was a time when I was like you. Her. Him. Driven. My mind not mine. She drove me. Do the sinks. Get the bread. Cut the grass.

158

Walk the dog. That shelf needs fixing. The car needs petrol. We've got no muesli. I want another pair of shoes. You haven't written that letter. Money.

Whose life is it? Inspector? Do you inspect? Do you look? Or do you decide? Do you see what you think?

Dick is wide-eyed.

Dick   Not bad, mate.

James smiles.

James   Inspector, I apologise for querying you. I'm sorry. It's not my business. No, I must not do that again. I'm sorry. I.

I must go now.

Nobody moves. Daks is dumb. You see James with new eyes. Dick is admiring the blue sky. Melinda says nothing. Cockatoo waits.

James   Thank you for listening to me.

You have a new appreciation of this man whom you invited. He is talking about something you've never considered. Until today you've seen characters lying on the pavement. You've not seen anyone like him as a person. Just dross. A throwaway. Discarded. A piece of jetsam lost overboard. But he's not. He's cultured. Calm. Well spoken. He has dignity. You rather like him and it seems he's about to disappear from your life, to merge again into the wasted masses.

You   James?

James   Yes.

You   Will you stay in touch?

James   How can I do that?

You watch as James walks quietly towards the towering buildings that surround the park. You turn to Melinda. James returns.

James   Did you ever hear about Diogenes?

Daks   Who?

James   He was a philosopher. He lived in a barrel.

Daks   What?

James   Well, that's the story they tell. He was Greek.

Daks   A bloody foreigner, then.

James   If you like. He lived a long time ago.

Daks   So, why are you telling me? Do you think we've got time to waste?

James   Exactly. That's it. Precise. Time to waste. Which is a pity. You see, I have time, just like you yourself, like my friend here and my new acquaintance here on the grass. We all have time. Isn't it marvellous? Time, as the world turns and the sun turns and the moon and the stars. Truly marvellous. I watch. Because people, they also turn. From young to old. They make mistakes, they tell lies, they seek truth, they want money, things, cars, new clothes, holidays, seaside, cruise ships, booze, especially booze, drugs, caffeine. Satisfaction, which they can't get.

Daks   Mr Robinson! Enough. I'm not here to listen to you.

James   No, sir, of course not. No, Inspector, I'll be on my way. Excuse me, I talk too much. It always was a fault. Talk, talk, talk. But consider.

No. I've said enough. Just consider.

Goodbye.

You have never thought like this before. What serendipity made you sit beside him? What prompting made you pull him to his feet? He has so much to impart. Wisdom, not just knowledge. If you had the courage to follow him. So many possibilities.

You   **My!**

Daks   **A crank.**

You think you will. But you don't. It wouldn't be a very good idea to criticise the Inspector. It wouldn't even be an idea at all. You did think it, though. You don't like him. You like Melinda. You like James too but he has gone. You probably will never see him again. And he's got your suit. Well, you gave it to him. What an extraordinary character. Could you? Sit and watch. Maybe you'd better not try and answer that. You know you couldn't so why even consider the possibility. He's a rarity, a one-off, a prophet, a holy man, saint.

Don't kid yourself. He's no more saintly than you are. And as for Dick, lying there, gazing. He's not watching, he's just idle. James has gone.

You   **Melinda, shall we go?**

Daks   **Not so fast.**

Melinda says nothing. She, too, is mesmerised by James. She watches in admiration as he walks away. She does not hear Mr Daks beside her.

Daks   **You are not out of my clutches. Not yet. I might not bother about him. But you. You are grating on my nerves. I'm raw. You…**

You   **Obfuscate, sir.**

Daks   **What? What the hell is that?**

Melinda   **He shrugs you off. Get's in your way. Obstreporous. Nuisance.**

Daks   Don't I know it.
Cockatoo wilts.

Chapter 17
DICK

The park, the square
You, Dick

There has to be a way to resolve this. You don't think you are guilty of anything. However, Daks does, and Daks is relentless. Perhaps one way might be to get Cockatoo to divulge the truth. The problem, of course, with this approach is that nobody understands what the bird says. At least, that is the assumption you are making. For the time being. So to speak. Irony. You speak. Does cockatoo? He certainly comments. Frequently. And not always in right ordering. Wretched bird.

Scrub that thought. Being rude isn't going to help. Appealing to his better nature might. Perhaps there's someone else.

You   What would you say, Dick?

Well, nobody understanding the bird is not quite true. Another bird would. Especially if they're the same species.

You   Have you ever seen a cockatoo, Dick?

Dick   A what?

You   A bird. White. Sort of yellow crest. Bit like a parrot. Talks a lot.

Dick   D'you mean the one you killed in the zoo?

You   Who told you that?

Dick   Common knowledge. The story's all over the place.

You are stumped, annoyed, cross. Are there no secrets? Is nothing sacred?

You   Well, for your information, Dick, whatever you've heard, it's not true. I did not, emphatically not, kill any bird, least of all a cockatoo, in the zoo. OK?

Dick   OK.

You   So how did you hear that story?

Dick thinks for a while. Shrugs his shoulders.

Dick   Dunn. Maybe in the paper.

This has to stop. This falsehood is going to destroy you. Daks will prove something, God knows what. You'll be banged up for murder, all on a trumped up charge that leaks all over the place. What to do?

You   I thought you were going home.

Dick   I was. But if you need help, I'll stay.

You   Thanks.

Dick   No problem. How about we go back to the beginning.

You   Where was that?

Dick   The survey? When we did that column. The one they thought was leaning.

You   The survey? D'you think something happened there?

Dick   Dunno. Might have. We could just retrace and see where it takes us. Or you.

You   OK.

Dick   Let's go then. The tube's over there.

You emerge from the Underground at the edge of the square. It looks just as it always has done. Stupid column, topped by even more stupid statue. Stupid lions growling at everyone. Pigeons. Starlings. Fountains. Switched off. Stupid people, breadcrumbs, lovers, office workers, tourists. Litter. Ice cream. No sign of cockatoo.

Dick Is that one, on top? The feathers?

You Yes, I think so. Looks harmless enough.

But you don't think this is the beginning. There was something else that happened. Something else that came before the leaning, or not leaning, upright, or no longer upright, column. You struggle to remember but Dick has set off to explore. You follow him.

Dick This is where we were set up. I remember.

You Yes. And the other point was over there.

Dick Anything?

You Nothing.

You tell Dick to go home. You'll sort things out for yourself, so you thank Dick as he goes, leaving you on your own. First of all, though, you'll go back to Melinda. Melinda. Now. You wonder if she is a true friend, or someone who's in a giant conspiracy with the wily Daks. She was talking to him in the park. She wears a blue serge jacket, which could be a police uniform, or part of one. She was driving a police car when she picked you up. and she was kind enough to stop to allow you to fetch James and rescue him. and there's another question that you've got to answer or get some satisfaction over. Is James the down and out he seemed to be or another agent working for the state? He'd got your keys. Well, you have them back now, of course. But did he take the keys or what. And he's now smartly dressed in clothes that aren't the ones you lent him. So what happened to those. You don't particularly want them, they weren't ones you liked, but you hadn't thrown them out. You don't throw any old clothes out, they just accumulate like the newspapers and the magazines, the plates and saucepans. You really are quite a mucky person. But who cares if you're living on your own, what does it matter. Well, it does matter. To you as well. So you could change your ways. Especially after this episode. Banged on the head with a cactus. Betrayed. Lost. Homeless. Moneyless. Conned by a taxi driver. No that wasn't you. He was quite fair. Took you exactly to the right place. Buns. It wasn't bad, that one in the café. Plastic chair. You didn't kill the cockatoo.

Dick is still there.

You   I thought you were going home?

Dick   I was but I'm going to make sure you find your way back to that bird of yours. She's quite pretty, isn't she? Bit old for me, but you never know. Actually, I don't really care for the way she dresses. Prefer them more jazzed, know what I mean? A bit of tart. Fluff. You know?

You   No, Dick, I don't. That's enough commentary for now.

Dick   Sorry, boss.

You have another look round the square. You look up at the column. Rock solid. Bloody silly statue. Bloody silly feathers. They say it's got two eyes. No eye patch. Can't see anyway. Dead. Stone. Bronze, whatever. Good job it can't speak.

Dick   Nice legs, though. And her hair. I like that.

You   Dick, will you shut up, please?

Dick   Why?

You   You're talking about my girlfriend.

Dick   I know. She could be my girlfriend, too.

You   Haven't you got enough? The way you talk, anyone would think you had dozens, all trailing after you. Or you're chasing them. Ye Gods, Dick.

Dick laughs.

You despair. You like Dick but. You know you are free to stop worrying about him. You've told him to go home. That he hasn't is no longer your concern. His idea to come back to the square was marginally helpful but now you think about it what was the point. There wouldn't be any evidence. It wasn't ever going to be a place for reconstruction. You've seen the column and the statue. That's it. Time to move on. Dismiss Dick. Let him go. He's of no account.

And yet. Maybe he does have something that you lack. He's certainly sanguine. He has his faults, fair do, you know he's never going to listen to you telling him he'll never have enough money, but that isn't what he has to give you. He has an honesty in his chasing after the fairer sex that you definitely don't have. And he has a healthy disrespect for policemen and what they can do. Besides, he could be invaluable in his knowledge, his skills in getting into places that ought to be locked. Magic. He would never find himself at a loss of where to go. He'd just do it. No questions. No problem. Perhaps you could keep him a bit closer. Well, not a friend, no that would go too far. You'd have to keep a proper respect, a decent distance between you. Like not let him come into your flat. Open the door for you, maybe, but not inside. Show you the right sort of bird, as he calls them, have a laugh, a beer, too many, get drunk, fool around. A night in the cells to sober up. No you wouldn't really want that. Let him do it but not you yourself. Hey ho! Dick, what a guy!

No account. No that isn't true. He does have account. He has value. Not all of it you want, but some of it, something. You don't have to like him, but strangely, you do like him. he makes you laugh. He's got that carefree way. Even when he's gazing up at the sky. Not worrying about an approaching inspector. Stupid name. Why would anyone want to be saddled with a name like that? Daks. Badger. He is though, isn't he. Rooting around. Poking his snout into places he didn't ought to. Turning up grubs. Snuffling in the dark. Wretched man. What with Dick, and Daks.

You	Hey!
Dick	What?
You	No not you. I just thought of something.
Dick	Cor. You don't say.
You	Cheeky.
Dick	So?
You	Your name and that inspector. Your names both begin with a d.
Dick	Yes. And?
You	Nothing. Just thought. That's all.

D. That is where it began. That conversation that began in filth and ended nowhere. You are still alone. Or are you? And if Dick isn't D, and Daks isn't D, then who is?

You	Dick, could you do something for me, please?
Dick	Yes. What?
You	Go home!

Chapter 18
I AM SHADOW
Your head

You

I am vast. I encompass the universe. I contain all the stuff, the experiences, the events, the happenings, the feelings, the incidents that you could not cope with. All the stuff that you decided you would dismiss, discard, throw away, be free of, be unencumbered by. I am the dreams you would rather not remember. I am shadow. I contain your desires, your ambitions, your curiosity, so much you'd like to be able to do. I hold it all. In safe keeping.

Everything you dropped by the wayside. You dropped because it was too much, it hurt, it didn't fit with your ideal, it didn't match your image, your self-created picture of who you think you are. I came along behind and picked it up. All of it. Nothing is lost, nothing left behind. Everything I keep. As pristine as the day you left it, so you thought, on the dump, the tip, in the bin, the trashcan. Not mine, you said, nothing to do with me, I don't want it, you said. But oh yes, it's yours and I picked it up, collected it every little bit.

And when you're ready I'll give it back, present it to you. You'll be surprised. You'll be shocked. You'll grow. You'll understand. You'll welcome the gift. You'll treasure it. You'll cheer with relief. You'll cry. You'll dance. The earth will shine for you. The sky will be bright blue and the sea will sparkle. You'll hear the birds as you've never heard them before.

I am not your enemy. I am not your friend either. I have unlimited power. If you provoke me, I will retaliate. If you make bargains with me, I will hold you to account and it will not go well with you. Do not jest. Do not make promises or threats. Do not make statements that you will regret. I will ensure punishment. I will exact revenge. If you so much as dare to offer me your right eye to know who I am and what I hold, you will, by no accident, poke out your right eye. And I will not be blamed. Don't! Not ever. Don't play with me. I am not your enemy, but I am not your friend either. You may work alongside me, I will create an alliance with you. But you will always be beholden to me. For what I have for you is mine to hold and mine to dispense. It did belong to you and you chucked it out. Not for me you declared. Not mine. So I kept it. Now it is for me to decide when and if.

You search for me. You look around. You are sure you only have to turn quickly and I will be there. Not so. I cannot be seen. I am faceless. A sense that I am there behind you, always just out of reach. You cannot see me.

Look at Daks. Tenacious, perseverance. He's not called a badger for nothing. He'll keep at it till he roots out the truth. But you're scared of him. You want to run away from him. He did hurt you and that was gratuitous, quite unnecessary. But what is it that he holds for you? Pigheaded. Unintelligent. Not that.

You feel alone. But I will never desert you. You might say that never is too absolute. There must be room for change. But for me, to be always with you, never to leave you, it's true. To the end of your days, I will be your shadow. And your search for me, for your true self which will never be fully revealed. You will always want more meaning. Always need to discover your purpose. Do I feel sorry? Not a bit. It is the fate for every conscious person. Better that you had never been born? That isn't an option, not even worth considering, so now you have a choice, to be responsible. Well, that won't do, because in the matter of taking responsibility there is no choice. You can choose all sorts of things but not that. In the end you will be responsible. You can argue as much as you like. But that will do you no good in the end. Instead, examine your future. Not your past, not what has happened, not your regrets, your guilt, your shame: your future.

You don't think much of Dick. He's young, adventurous, boasting. You tire of trying to educate him, as you call it, but he's not interested like that. So why do you keep him? What does he offer you? What does he hold that you don't have?

And Melinda and James? You have a lot to discover. They are only clues. The truth I hold. Other people give pointers. What are the secrets you would never divulge? I know them. You cannot hide them from me. Violence, porn. Untidiness you know. But murder? Oh yes, it's here. I know you didn't kill the cockatoo but the thought that you dare not speak aloud is present within you. You pretend it isn't. I know it is. Go where you like, I am ever beside you.

I am not the master. I am not your servant. I am neither angel, nor devil. I am not God. I have no form. I cannot be seen. I have no voice. I am shadow. You want to know what sort of colour I am. You want to know an awful lot about me but I am not a person. I am shadow.

Chapter 19
HOME
Your flat
You, Daks, Melinda

You let yourself into your flat. It feels like nothing has changed. The plate is still on the draining board with James' note. His other note is still lying on the floor where you tossed it in disgust. There is no-one except you.

Of course, you are relieved to be home, but something has changed. Nothing physical but inside. Your soul has been affected. You are not worried about the possibility of Daks appearing and, strangely, you aren't worried about where Melinda might be. Though, of course, you don't want to lose her completely. Something else.

You are calm. At other times you might have paced through each room, checking, but not now. You go into the kitchen, put the plate where it lives. How James couldn't find that, God only knows. Never mind. Unimportant. Put the kettle on. Mug. Coffee. No milk. Black with some sugar. Quite nice like that. They say coffee is always better a bit sweet. Bitter. Any chocolate? Two pieces. In the silver paper. Nice. Coffee and chocolate. Really well together.

You savour the mixture. Melange. Nice word. Nice taste. A bit of quiet. Thank God, got rid of Dick. He can be a real nuisance sometimes. Good enough chap. Helpful. Willing. But all the same. He's only there to help. He's not your bosom friend. Melinda. Like her bosom. Nice word. Cuddly. Cosy. Nice tits. Mustn't call them that.

Boobs. Breasts. Bosom. Into the bosom of… Must be a saying like that. Can't remember what though. Ask Melinda, she might know. Come to think, I think it's into the bosom of Abraham. How silly. Unless you were gay. Who comes up with them? Sayings. Mottos. Do a lot of good. Do a lot of damage, too. Stops you working things out for yourself. Still, part of humanity. Can't stop it. Like history. Rolls on. Looking at the past. Helps you go on. Does it really? Not sure. Could be better. Not think of the past. Live forward. Aborigines say we have our backs to the future. Our fronts to the past. That's why we're always thinking about what's gone instead of what's next. Wonder where I heard that? Interesting observation. Sort of changes things.

Coffee cup, mug, empty. Needs washing up. No hot water. Put the timer on override. Soon be warm enough. Turn around. Me. Turn around.

The doorbell rings. You have a choice, ignore, go downstairs, look out of the window. Ignore is yesterday's way. You've turned around. Not going to ignore. It's rude anyway. And besides, it could be Melinda.

You look out of the window. Nobody to be seen. So, it's not anybody who's used to coming. They'd be standing on the pavement, looking up, waiting for you to open the window and chuck the key out to them. Somebody else. Maybe you know them. Do they know you?

The doorbell rings again. Still polite.

You go downstairs, taking extreme care to hold the keys in your hand and close the door very carefully behind you. Not going to do that again. Made one mistake. Not going to repeat the same thing. Stupid idiot. And yet, it wasn't actually you, was it. James took them. Why did he do that? Mistake. Just popping out. Thought they were his. No, the note looked more permanent. And he's there, dressed in new clothes, not your old ones.

You open the front door. Melinda and Daks. Together.

Daks   Emil Finch?

You   Yes.

Daks   I'm arresting you for the murder of Mr Albert Cockatoo.

You   What?

You wanted fame, not notoriety. You wanted to be in the papers but not this way. "Killer Gaoled." You can see them sitting in the tube, on the buses. Thank God. He's been caught. Won't do that again. Real evil. Horrible. Keep him locked up for a very long time. Thought he could get away with it. Buried the body. Cut it into little pieces. You can't escape the law. Clever, he thought he was. Not so clever now. Good riddance. Put him where he ought to be. In his place. Keep us safe.

Is this what happens when you tempt the shadow? You try to be honest and you end up getting the wrong thing. Hell instead of heaven. Or maybe it is notoriety you want. To be famous for anything. Even when it isn't true.

You   How d'you work that out? Albert. A bird perhaps. But Albert?

Daks muses for an instant but dismisses it just as instantly. If he makes mistakes they are of no consequence. He works out the truth and it is the truth. No question.

Daks   The body has been found in the canal where you dumped it. Mangled. Half decomposing. And it's been proved.

You   Body in the canal?

Daks	Come on, sir. It's no use arguing on the doorstep.
You	Melinda, are you in on this? Are you... You really are a copper, working with him, aren't you?

People are standing by, watching. It's just like that day at the zoo, for heaven's sake.

You	Melinda, I thought you were my friend. Are you working for him or what? I thought you liked me. I thought you were...
	I'm gasping.
Melinda	I'm sorry. I did try to persuade Mr Daks that it could be a mistake, someone else, not a murder at all but he's shown me the proof and it's incontrovertible. The court will accept it.
You	Ye gods!
Daks	I think it would help if you called your solicitor.
You	I will.

Melinda, of all people. With the inspector standing right next to her, you can't even talk to her. She was so helpful. She waited for you. She picked you up. How come, you didn't take note when she drove up in a police car? Idiot. The trouble is you take too much on trust. Of course, you should have realised when she disappeared. James. Is he OK, someone to be trusted, someone you can rely on? Who can you trust? Not even yourself. Fame, you wanted. Not like this. People watching. There'll be press photographers next. Damn it. Get your face in the paper. Desperate criminal, nabbed. What a joke if it wasn't so awful.

Wonder what'll happen. Up in court. Be a bag of nerves, sweat breaking out. Tell the truth. So help me God. Whole truth. Nothing but. Will they believe. And then locked in a cell. Steel door with no handle. Guards peeping.

Could be a woman judge. Like Melinda.

No, not like her. Someone fierce. A Harridan. After your guts. Keep hammering on until you give in.

You   Melinda, I know you're with the inspector, but can I talk to you, please?

Melinda   No.

Chapter 20
COURT
A courtroom
Cockatoo, Daks, Nelson, Melinda, a Keeper

You watch a procession. Call the next witness. A man in green overalls enters with Cockatoo on his shoulder. The judge, a lady, hard as nails, framed in grey, cloaked in scarlet, questions whether you are permitted to bring pets into the courtroom. The man replies that he is not the person who is to be questioned, but the bird itself. The judge looks askance. How can a bird testify. How would anybody trust which bird it was. All birds look the same. Take the bird away. The court will not hear such a ridiculous argument. The bird is not fit: it's not the same bird.

Cockatoo   Same bird! Same bird! Same bird!

Cockatoo has dignity. He stands proud on the zoo-keeper's shoulder. His plumage is beautifully white. The crest on his head shines golden yellow in the sombre atmosphere of the courtroom. The jury look grey. The judge looks furious. You look on in horror. What on earth can a bird do. No-one can understand cockatoo, except perhaps another cockatoo.

You   Do your trick, bird. Pretend to be dead and rise again like Christ from the tomb. Fall down, play doggo. Do your thing.

You're too far away to offer another bite of stone hard Chelsea bun. You rely on your power of imagination. Cockatoo is sullenly superior, silently untouchable. He

179

digs his claws into the zoo-keeper's shoulder. The keeper winces.

You look at Cockatoo, intently.

You Come on you stupid bird, say something, do something. Don't just leave me here to be banged away. You know, you know that I know you know. I know you know I didn't kill you. I know your tricks. Fall off, get up when nobody's looking. Fly off, go and talk to that statue. Eyes wide open. All seeing, but not God, no god forbid, not that omnipotent. Actually quite the opposite. Hardly potent at all. Not at all. Stuck up. Nose in the air. Couldn't get it up if he tried. Bloody heroes. Make a column, stick him on top, call it done, worship him forever. Or not, till he comes tumbling down. Rewrite history. What a fable. Make everyone believe it's true when you all know it jolly well isn't. How come? Don't you use your intelligence. Work things out for yourself. Come on bird. Sing or do something. Don't just sit there. Stand there. Sharp claws. Grasping beak. Pity the bloke in the green. Come specially from the zoo, to carry you here. Can't you fly on your own? Or would that be too much to ask? Sing! Speak!

Cockatoo cocks a sly eye. Winks. Haughty.

He is the key witness, isn't he? Must be. It's the crime you're charged with. Call the next witness. Enter your nemesis. The badger. Tall, moustache, bald. He's not a witness. He didn't see anything. He simply presumed on flaky evidence which was hearsay, saw something, must be you.

These witnesses are all you have. Nobody else cares.
You've left your flat which is now re-occupied and you
know by whom. Even your girlfriend. Melinda please.
Appear. Be kind, like you were. The lady in the fur coat.
The old Mrs Dinkins, Johnkins, dead in her grave. Cups
of tea with an extra one for the guest who was never
invited. You left her out in the cold. Appalling behaviour.
Tried to kiss her. Insisted it was right. In full public view.
Thank God, she declined. Cockatoo would have blabbed.
Blurted it out. Told the statue. Dick. He knew. How ever
did you get to this state?

You started by asking questions. You wanted to find out
a name, who you were, who you are. You were alone and
now that you're surrounded you're still not satisfied. You
have been given so many clues and still you refuse to
listen. You want to know if it will ever end. Will you ever
discover your purpose, the reason for your life, why
you're here, why you were born and the answer is so
simple. It's so simple because there isn't one, not in the
manner of your faulty logic that demands cause and
effect, that wants something to ease the distress in your
mind. The answer you seek does not exist, only existence
itself exists. You were born to be, not for any ulterior
motive. You are dark and light. This courtroom is in your
mind. There is nothing real about it. The figures who
parade in front of you, your witnesses, are real enough,
each one of them is genuine, except perhaps. No, even
Cockatoo is real. He too with the white feathers, symbol
of giving in, too much conscience, too much objection,
just as now you object to being shown what you don't
want to see.

The inspector is giving his evidence. Such a lie. He never
observed, only heard, hearsay, see saw. Believed. The
taxi driver was good to him. Took him to Trumpet Street,

not Triumph as he had asked and let him see the name he wanted. Such a shrewd observer, just like you. Unwilling to see what really is. That you are who you are, nothing more, nothing less. A body like every other living thing. Just a body. Only your conscience has turned you in on yourself, made you a coward. Will you, like Hamlet, destroy the very ones you love? Melinda, your friend, your love, the one who cares for you, who deeply wants you to enjoy your life. And all the others who want no more.

Daks　　I saw him shoot the weapon through the bars of the cage. I saw the bird fall dead to the floor.

Guilty, ashamed. Your secrets exposed. You are the only one who can't see your shadow. It's plain for everyone else to see. And why should that upset you. Your shadow is not your enemy. You are.

Cockatoo drops dead to the floor. Uproar. Arms in the air. The zoo-keeper shrieks. But you know it's only a trick. Cockatoo lies lifeless. Beak half open. Inspector Daks can't believe his eyes. But then he does believe all sorts of other things so it is of little account. Don't dismiss. He has power, which you don't. Not yet. Dick laughs. The statue shudders. Cockatoo winks his eye.

Nelson　　Get up!

Melinda is standing by your side. You are thrown into doubt again. Is she or is she not on your side? In the police force? Or your friend?

Melinda　　Did you see that?

You　　Well, not exactly something you could avoid.

And look, my hands are empty. Not one sign of a Chelsea bun, half eaten or otherwise.

Melinda　　Were they nice?

You   Not bad, especially the one I had in the café.

Cockatoo vanishes. The zoo-keeper had turned away to look at Daks. You looked at Melinda. Daks looked at the ceiling in despair. And – gone. The hint of a flash of white and gold. Gone. Pandemonium. People rush around, checking doors, windows, fanlights. Except you. You expected this, you smile. Melinda notices.

Melinda   Why are you laughing? Did you know this was going to happen?

You turn around.

You   Look, no hands.

You lift your pullover away from your middle.

You   Look, nothing.

You pull your pockets inside out. Fluff and a hard snot of chewing gum. The bird has birdied. It is not here. Disparu. Hole in one. Though how, through which hole, by what route, nobody is clear. Floor, ceiling, chimney, there isn't one.

Daks approaches you with menace.

Daks   Do I have to add kidnap to murder?

You   No, sir. Besides,...

But you think better than to riposte with a jibe. William Daks aroused is dangerous. You think better but your impulsive self is not so circumspect.

You   Shall we go to the café for a tea and a Chelsea bun?

The inspector's face turns purple. Melinda restrains his hand, which makes you wonder, yet again, whose side is she on. You regret your quick wit.

Liar. You love it.

So, what are you going to do? You can't run away, that would surely bring the full force on top of you. You can't ask Melinda directly. Or you could. You could appeal to Dick. Whatever for? Cecile is dead. D. Not Dick, not Daks, D.

You are not alone. There are people all around you. The zoo-keeper approaches.

Keeper   You've seen this happen before, haven't you?

You   Yes.

Keeper   Do you know how he does it? The bird, I mean.

You   Not a clue.

Keeper   It's a trick, though, isn't it?

You   Oh, sure of it. I mean you can't... I mean resurrection isn't a reality. And it is the same bird. Though, I don't know how I know that. He winked at me when he was playing dead. It's a good trick, though, isn't it? I tell you, what. You aren't the witness, are you?

Keeper   No. I'm just the carrier.

You   So I could be free to leave, couldn't I?

Keeper   You are free. You could just apologise and say you're going to see if you can retrieve the bird... Cockatoo.

You   I'm on it.

Now, you are alone. D.

Chapter 21
CONVERSATION RESUMED
The dining room
A Chorus, You, D

There is blood in the air. Fine red droplets cloud our vision. They don't go away. No matter how long. Menace remains, always live, always present, buried perhaps but never inaccessible. Like the drops that fall danger rises. Are we destined to live with it? Forever, oh God.

You   D! I am waiting. A response, an explanation, a story, something, please, I beg you.

Silence. We wait. The world waits. Be quiet!

You   My tears are red. You tell me nothing. How am I to know. Do I have to dig, to uncover, to realise the secrets of your past? Make them real. Out of a story which you never have the grace to tell me.

D   So why continue to probe so deeply?

You   You tell me nothing. A delicatessen, a train, a telephone. End.

Silence. D. Nix. Mouth shut. Not even a smile. We wait. He tries again. Futile. Is he stupid or what?

You   Yes, shit happens, I know. So why not be out with it? You must be able to say something. Please.

D   Because I tried to live beyond it, beyond its clutches of panic, desperation, fear. You have no idea.

You   I would if you spoke.

185

D   I did.

When? He spoke? Did we miss something or is it him, that he didn't want to hear? Is it his ears closed or ours? His mind set hard or ours? Not paying attention. Listen. D is speaking.

D   Perhaps, you were looking after yourself.

You   I was growing, finding my way, my path, my future.

D   And?

You   Not and, but. My future was not independent of your past, of the story that is my inheritance, as well as yours.

Will you not wipe my tears?

D   And merge them into my tears. There's enough salt. We don't need any more. There are piles of it already. We have both wept.

You   Then let us look for a way, a channel. Let me begin to understand you, your life. What motivates you. What happened to you that you don't talk.

D   I did talk.

He is lost in his own little world. There is only his aching body. Nothing else. No-one beside him. The pain is everything. He sees blackness. The sun is shining and the sky is pitch dark. No light penetrates into the depth of his soul. We see him struggle. Somehow he must rise. Against lethargy.

You   Maybe you didn't dare.

D   Oh, I dared all right. And my throat refused. My tongue decided not.

You   Then you drove me in a direction I didn't want to go.

D   Never. You vilify me. You put words on my lips. You are your own person.

See. Silenced into submission.

You   D?

D   Fair enough. We shall converse as man to man.

Oh hell. Look what is happening. It is his turn to be grown up. It is a mutual exercise. One alone cannot speak into a void. Without reflection, without to and fro, without listening. Don't let the muck and the filth get bunged up. Only so much you can throw into a cess pit before it overflows. Disgusting, the smell, the putrid mouldering fly ridden mess.

Stop. Do not descend. You've been there and it's hell. Why venture again. Look away. Leave. You only imagine you are hanging naked on a hook. It isn't true. The wickedness is of your own making. You can choose. Life or death. D is offering. Speak. Converse. Wake up. D is still there, patient. You can accuse but who is the guilty one?

You   Perhaps it isn't just me by my own devices. Perhaps you, too, are looking for ways, searching for the pimpernel, the juice of the flower that heals, that restores to life, to wholeness.

D   I chose wine. It tastes better than flower juice. But let that be. I didn't want you to get drunk.

You   I'm sorry. I didn't mean to.

D   There you go again. This is just you. Where am I in this conversation?

Spite in his veins. In his speech. In his thoughts. Anything not to do as D says. Anything to think differently. As if he could. As if he was so utterly divorced from D. And yet here we are. We see him. Separate from D? No. With D!

D   Well then, I will talk.

Over his gravestone! Where his skeleton is all that will remain. A name, D. Born. Died. Is that all there is. Such a life. Disposed of, a name, a date, a place. Another date, another place. How can a whole life be condensed into so few words?

Wait! For goodness sake, wait.

D   My, you really do think the whole world revolves around you. You're not the cause of everything that happens. You're not to blame for the state of the world. Neither am I. It's just history. A blip. A minor disturbance in the flux of the universe. A storm that rages and then all is quiet. A lightning strike. A lot of noise. All designed to scare you. Oh sure, God does that you know. No uncertain terms, thunderbolt at the ready, chuck it down at your feet. A little firecracker. Bang, whizz. Jump. Bang. Sorry about that old boy. Couldn't help it. A bit of fun. Nothing more. Did it scare you? Well, well, well, who would have thought it. A mighty man like you. Come, come. Be brave. Pick yourself up. No harm done.

You   A blip? Minor? Not many dead? Is that why you won't talk?

D   I keep telling you, I did talk.

You   Well, not about what mattered to me.

D   You see, there you go again. You're so selfish. It's not all you.

Hell. It is him, what he wants. What if he has imagined the whole scenario? A play that is re-enacted inside his head? His own private theatre where he sits as audience and actor. Night after night. An awful tragedy that is played to its bitter end but is never fulfilled. While we stand in the wings. Waiting. Or at the edge of the stage, watching, listening, taking note. It could be worse, a comedy of errors, played upon him by a clown. The joke's on him. But it's not a joke. Surely not. It doesn't make us laugh. Not at all. We weep, we tremble, we shudder.

Did he pay good money to get a ticket to enter? Did he pass some audition to be allowed to tread out onto the boards, to harangue? Is he the only person in the auditorium? Is he the protagonist? Then who the antagonist? D? Himself? Two characters in one persona. Is this wholly an internal struggle? We are powerless. We stand at the edge. We cannot intervene. We are forbidden to prevent folly, only to watch. Does D even exist or is he a figment of his imagination. A leftover. A phantom memory? He does not know. And still the fine red droplets drip. Blood in the air. It clouds our eyes.

You   I thought it was my place to forgive you, D. Now, it seems, it is me to say sorry. I have maligned you, framed you as the persecutor, accused you of secrecy, of lies. If anyone is to forgive I have to ask it of you. How can I?

Confusion. Worse than before for the nightmare doesn't stop, doesn't cease because he has reassessed, examined, queried.

D   You are puzzled. You are frowning. Your brow is lined.

You   Will you tell me your story?

D	On one condition.
You	Accepted.
D	What, without argument? You'll let me tell you only what I am going to tell? You won't quiz, you won't probe, you won't demand more than I am going to say?
You	Is that because you aren't willing?
D	You see, immediately, there you go. What is this willing? Why do you question my motives? Already it's lopsided. For sure, yes, I have motives, so do you.
You	So, D, let us begin with our honour.
D	Honour? Are you implying you have integrity? That you are pure, undefiled, blameless, without sin. Even your face is not symmetrical. On one side you smile and your eye twinkles. On the other impatience, fury even.
You	I am crushed.
D	No! Not crushed. No person deserves that, not me, not you, not anyone. To be crushed, to admit defeat, to lose the argument, the war, turn tail and flee, pursued by a bear. Is that what you think?
You	Then why, tell me, please, why, D, am I so unsatisfied?
D	I don't know.
You	No, I suppose not. You cannot answer what could only be my question.
D	Then, listen. I left home.

Long pause. We have nothing to add. We remain here, without comment. Drowning in red. Keeping our heads up. Stop talking. Listen.

| You | Is that it? |
| D | No. |

Again. Nothing. Now we have lost our voice. Gargle. Dettol. Liquorice. Quick. Don't miss the next instalment.

D	I made my own home.
You	And that's it.
D	Yes.
You	And that's what you claim you told me.
D	In effect, yes.
You	So, you didn't tell me.
D	Not in words, no.

We knew it. D was lying. The toad. Wait! We must not judge.

| You | We seem to be stuck. |
| D | We do. |

The truck is an exhibit in a museum. With a little notice in polite black and white text. The bare minimum of explanation. This. Part of the transport. Left Berlin for Riga. 19th of January. Deported. 1942. Death. People read. They look. An empty truck that's all. Sanitised. Immobile. Boards of wood. No sweat. No tears. Not even a whiff of disinfectant ready for the next one thousand souls. In hell now. Cattle wagons for people. Human beings. Mothers, fathers, names, lives, dignity. Livelihoods all gone. The shop she ran. The delicatessen where he savoured sausage. Bright red peppers. Plum sweets covered in velvet chocolate.

| You | The tears I shed, are they mine alone? |
| D | No. I have wept too. In my time. |

Do you remember the Swiss Chocolate. Big bars. Milk chocolate. Hazelnut. I brought them for you.

You   I remember. Thank you.

Twelve years of murder. Gas ovens. Rifle shots. Torture. Starvation. Yellow stars. Cattle trucks. Crammed in with nowhere to rest in a train that clanks and shunts, jolts and stays silent for hours on end in the dead of night.

You   You don't cry?

D   No. What for?

I've wept enough. To fill the oceans. Then I dried my tears and poured myself a glass of wine.

Waiter!

Bring us Schnitzel. Chicken soup. A little salad.

Come, sit. Your napkin.

No. He cannot. He cannot be polite while this is still raw in his heart. How long? How long Lord must he endure? Are You not his protection? What bloody use is that? Why didn't You stop them? You. He called You omnipotent. You called us to witness to Your immensity. You demanded that we ensure he is aware, them both, all of them. Throughout the world, a story of terror. You made us stand and watch. We observed. We noticed. We screamed. Stop, we said. We yelled. And You did nothing. You. You were powerless. Until it burnt itself out of its own accord. Twelve years. That was all but enough to kill millions. A wasteland of grief. And still we are unrelieved of our duties. Bound to You by invisible strings we obey. We stand. Testimonials. Is that all that is left?

D	You hesitate?
You	I am angry.
D	Then slam the door shut.
You	What?
D	Slam it. Hard! Give it everything you've got. Power. Don't for one moment hold even the tiniest part of your being in reserve.
	You see, it's just a blip.
	Bon appetit.
	The sound reverberates. Across the globe. People hear it. And then it gets fainter. People sense a whisper. And it's vanished. Thin air. A blip.
You	I can still hear it. Clearly.
D	I don't doubt you. You always were hypersensitive.
You	And you weren't?
D	I decided.

We look at him. We are astonished. He looks at D. He is astonished. We cry, we weep, we bawl our eyes out, sob, sniff.

Hankie!

Where were You by accident of fate that insemination created them of all people. So many millions of possibilities and they came out, emerged bawling, gasping, wet. Why him? Why D? Was there no other possibility? Were You present? Or did You cover Your eyes from the face of the earth? Moses was right. You hid.

A combination by the laws of chance, of physics. Each one unique. Every living thing that ever there was, never to be repeated, not now, not then, not next. Different. One and one alone. Years that pass flashed over in a few seconds of imperfect memory. The feelings, the images, the sensations. A story. One that You conjured. Out of nihil. Chaos You turned into order. You fashioned rules. You created structure. The story of their lives, how they came to be, who nurtured them, brought them out of the soft, dark, wet, silent wombs, into the classroom, into the streets, the factories, the fields, forests, magazines, slaughterhouses, churches, temples where they worshipped You. Why on earth? Whatever did You do for them? You hid. How could You?

You   And you say it will pass. The world will forget?

D   Certainly. Maybe not in my lifetime or in yours. What do you think? That people can afford to let their lives be dominated by something that happened?

You   Twelve years. To end in a pit with no name, no stone. Is that not something?

D   A blip. A discontinuity. An aberration. There are many cemeteries. Nobody can remember everyone. Think back over the centuries, the thousands of years. How many people have names? You have no idea.

Come, the soup is getting cold.

Not bad. Tasty.

Of course, everybody did have a name. We're all individuals. And we have to tell so-and-so I love you or don't do that or can we please.

You   Please don't slurp. I hate that.

D   What? Oh, sorry. If you eat, yourself, it won't bother you.

| You | You're heartless. |
| D | Not at all. Just hungry. |

Omniscient, all seeing, nothing hid from their eyes. Our eyes. And You stood by. Your hands in Your pockets. Theirs are my hands You yelled. Our hands. And we did nothing. Powerless, befuddled by lies, damned lies. Hate. Bullying. Telling it not like it is but besmirching the good name. We listened and You hooked them with Your line and sinker. No use. We who are about to die. Taken in. Hoodwinked. And yet we may not die. You have decreed us to be immortal. Always present. Sentinels. Guarding Your creation.

Forget it. Look. He is lifting his spoon.

You	This soup's nice.
D	Just like mother made!
You	I miss her.
D	Of course. So do I.

Forget? He is lying. One prod, one word, a glance, a hint. It'll come flooding back, blocking the arteries, filling his gorge. His brain hurts. He must be in agony. It's easy to press his button.

D	Waiter. A bottle of red. The best you have.
You	Are you turning this into a celebration?
D	Yes, why not? You are alive and so am I. The dead are dead and there's nothing you can do to change it. The toast has always been "LaChaim!". Why should it be any different now? "To Life!" I have no power to bring her back. You only think you do. Go on, go down to Hades. Plead with Pluto. Let me have her, please. And he'll say "no problem." Only there is a problem because if you once look back to

check she's following, she'll vanish forever. And then where will you be?

You — You're callous.

D — Yes. And next, you'll say you hate me.

And I assure you, you will look back.

Cheers. Chin chin.

One voice says go. And another he may never forget. One voice pulls back. One voice change. Safety is the best policy. Stick with what you know. Don't venture where you've never been. Enjoy. Get drunk. You'll never have another chance. This is it. Make the most of it. It won't come back. Lose this now, lose it forever. Pull. Push. Drink. Sober. Fear. Who cares? What the hell! She's calling you. The grave, the grave, the grave.

You — La'Chaim!

Curtain.

Chapter 22

CHEER

Outside the court
You, Melinda

Melinda is standing outside the courthouse. She is still wearing the blue serge. Inspector Daks is beside her.

You   Can I talk to you, please?

Melinda   Of course.

You fumble for the words you need to ask her. Instead, you tell Daks how grateful you are that he gave in. And in return Daks sneers. He hasn't given up. Despite the bird's trick he still thinks you're guilty.

Cockatoo sniggers. You've heard it many times. There must be some motive behind the unseemly comments. There must be some reason why you are continually mocked. You don't want to know but your shadow already does. If you're going to find your true identity you'll have to give in. What is truth. Pilate. A figment of the imagination. Plato's unachievable perfection. Damn the man. Cursed now through history. Striving for precision. For a sense which has no nuance. Truth. It doesn't exist. Judges come and go. Daks swears blind he knows. Cockatoo falls dead and disappears and still you don't understand. Has your conversation with D meant nothing? Was it all a sham? You forgave him, but you lied. Or did you tell the truth. Swear upon the mighty word of God, I shall do no other. Bible. Right hand. You don't tell anyone you're left-handed. The oath never counted. You have perjured yourself. No crime has been committed. Cockatoo flies free, never was murdered, not least by a Chelsea bun. Stuck in a cage he might have been. Was he not always free? Across the city. Park, square, fountains, trees, rooftops, statue, taxis, buses, chimneys, aerials. The sky's the limit. Unbound. Uncaged. But helped by a keeper in a green overall. You cheat, too, bird. Doesn't everyone. Learn it young, never own up. Pretence is fun. Deceit is a grand game of play. Mum against Dad, sister against brother. Till it becomes a habit as strong as stainless steel. Chains too thick to cut. Entangled. A Gordian knot of astonishing proportions, built of tiny lies woven into bigger lies, twisted with whoppers. Truth might not exist but lies certainly do.

Is it possible, having forgiven D, you could now find some forgiveness in your own heart for yourself. That way lies salvation. Confession of sins. Absolution. Go into a dark corner and speak to the one who hears all. No priest, just you and the all-knowing, all-seeing. No matter such omnipotence, such omniscience failed to halt the tragedy of the murder of your ancestors. Your family. Jesus was Jewish too. Killed. Mocked. Tortured. It doesn't stop, not ever. It may be a lull but it will continue, now and for ever.

In this interlude between the blips, live. For today. For the present. Be the one who you are meant to be. Question not. Cease the endless probing to which there never will be an answer. The response is always the same. I am that I am. Enigmatic. Palindromic. Am I that I am? The reply is emphatically, Yes, none other. It could not be anything other than I am. You are. Your body tells the truth. There, it does exist. Hidden deep within you. Sinews, vessels, muscles, spleen, nerves. Bones excited by drumming. Blood moved by the sound of the flute. Your nerves twanging to the buzz of the violin string. All one.

Moving, keeping you alive, until one day you die. But not yet. Today you are here. Alive. You need nothing else. Propose to her! Offer her companionship. Yours to give freely to her. Leave the badger to his imagination. Forget Dinkins, Donkins, Johnkins. She is dead but not Melinda. If Trevor Jones existed does it matter? Let Dick be Dick. Let Cockatoo enjoy his flights. Fancy. Taste. A Chelsea bun to remember and savour. The time is past. Be now into the future from today, the present. Exclaim, halleluia. Out of excelsis comes Deo.

You are a man. A person. You are not God. Though you are divinely ordained. A spiritual being, here on earth to have the experience of a lifetime. This is it. There's nothing else. Manifested in a body, with heart and mind and soul, with strength and power, weakness and failings. Mistakes will occur. Trips, falls, tumbles, downsides. Up you get. Dust yourself off. Take the next step. Be here now. When you die, you will not be. No, you. Nothing. Into the ether. Dust to dust. All your molecules and atoms dispersed into the vastness of the universe. Enjoy it now while you can. You have time left, years to pass. Go while you can. Walk, run. Sit still.

Do not question the tree of knowledge. Do not test the tree of good and evil. Do not be tempted. Satan is everywhere.

You   Melinda, will you come with me?

Eat an apple, or a fig, but beware expulsion. Tread between the wandering rocks, tread carefully. But never doubt that you can. You have strength around you, like a golden robe. Optimism will lead you forwards where the opposite will drag on your heels. But like Candide, you may well find that great achievement will be dropped at the wayside. To cultivate your garden will be your worthwhile and self-esteem enhancing occupation. A spade, a glass of water, fresh beans.

Melinda looks at Daks. She smiles, shakes his hand and leaves him. Then she turns back to him. He grimaces. And she comes to you.

Melinda I've resigned.

You Just like that? Don't you have to write a formal letter or something?

You walk together away from the courthouse leaving Inspector Daks staring into space.

Cockatoo cheers.

Chapter 23
LIFE
Your flat
You, Melinda

You open the door to your flat at No 41. Something is different. James has been here. The clothes you lent him are folded neatly. Returned to you. But no note this time. An implied thank you but this makes you cross. He should have left you a note. You know he is grateful, but you want to hear him say so.

Melinda has gone into the kitchen. It's chilly. A window has been left open. She looks out, then closes it. She tidies a mug from the draining board, washes two plates left in the sink. Why two plates? She wipes the table down. A newspaper lying on one of the chairs. The tea-towel is disgusting. Stained, frayed at the edge, the hanger ripped. A saucepan on the cooker, dried baked beans. The top of the cooker spattered with grease. She sighs. How can you live in such a mess? Don't you care about yourself? A pair of what look like soiled underpants in the corner. She goes to pick them up, stops herself. If she's going to live with you, there's going to be a lot of changes to be made. Domestic bliss! More like constant rows and shouting matches. How many times do I have to tell you? You never listen. You do. You put things away. You don't leave things lying around. You do the washing up. Little mistakes, they're not important. You can live with them, so could she. She can't.

You are standing bewildered in the sitting room, staring out of the window at the tops of the plane trees as if you've never noticed them before. Your books, your letters, the bills you haven't paid, the bills you have paid, the fliers, circulars, newspapers, magazines, Chinese takeaways, pizzas delivered to your door, Indian takeaways, unopened envelopes, demands, exhortations, come-ons, bank statements, notes, business cards, paper, paper, paper, white, brown, grey. Your whole life laid out in untidy piles, scattered correspondence. Words that once meant something, words that have no meaning at all, numbers, pound signs, ink, blue, black, grey. Whoever invented printing, writing, drawing, graving, whatever were they thinking of? Did they imagine the amount of waste they were creating? Packaging, plastic, bags, polythene, wrappers, tins, jars, bottles, pots, lids, screw tops, corks, snap, twist, grasp, wrench, struggle, click, break. So much paraphernalia in order to make you a human being. Not satisfied with a body. You daren't go into the bedroom. Bedclothes, duvet, blanket, trousers, socks, pants, shirts, jacket, ties. Discarded, motheaten, smart, worn, frayed, ironed, smooth, spots, washed, crumpled, bits of breakfast, dust, cobwebs, flakes of skin, hair.

Dead.

Better to live.

Melinda   Shall we do some tidying up?

You'd much rather find out what she was doing with the police, why she seemed to be Daks's sidekick, why she so obviously came to help you, is still helping you. Where she lives, too? You never asked her. But how to begin, how to ask without implying you don't believe her? She's taken off her jacket. A white blouse underneath which doesn't look anything like a uniform. Come to think of it the jacket doesn't either but there she was in deep conversation with Daks and driving a police car. That was kind. And she waited for you. Sitting on the bench waiting for you. You sit down at the kitchen table.

You   No, there's more important things to do.

She sits down beside you. Smiles. You can't ask her. She's much too nice.

You   Are you going to stay?

Melinda   What?

You   I mean. Sorry!

Melinda   No, that's OK. Just a bit sudden.

You need a drink. No milk in the fridge. Coffee. Black. Ring for a takeaway. Could be a Chinese. Jasmine tea. Do they deliver? Maybe you have to make your own. Pity. Or could be a salty lassi. You quite like that. Cools the chilli. Don't like things so hot. Nice bit of mango chutney. Or spare ribs. Eat with your fingers. Get all mucky. Scooping the rice out of bowls. Stupid, pretending to be native. Just use a spoon instead. Why isn't there a takeaway for steak and kidney pie? Fish and chips though. Mushy peas. Coke. Fizz makes you burp. Not very polite with Melinda next to you. Can't burp quietly. Big throaty noise. Revolting, really. Rots your teeth as well. Does wonders for the spirit. Or a glass of wine. Get a bit drunk. Try it with her. Fumble. Is the bed made? Probably just left it the way you always do. She might, though. Not sure. you'd have to play it. Softly, softly. Well, she did come back home with you. That's the first thing. Pretty neat that.

You   Do you like Chinese? Indian?

Melinda   Are you inviting me?

You're throbbing. Excited. Smile.

You   I'll ring for a pizza. Four seasons. With an egg on top. One each. OK?

Melinda   Smashing.

You do nothing. You know you've got the chance of a lifetime to make this into a happy ending. You and Melinda sitting at your kitchen table, together. And at the back of your mind, doubts and questions that won't go away. Why should misfortune be dispelled because something new has happened? Why shouldn't tragedy be your fate? Why shouldn't Melinda's resignation be a fake, a ploy to draw you back into the prison of your soul? You smile but you are scared it's false. And you know Melinda knows. Don't they ever go away? Can you never be free? Look forward. The sun is shining. The rain is gentle. The breeze refreshes. It's not a gale. When the snow falls it's a covering of magic. It's not a disaster. You will not trip or skid or fall. The seasons turn, each one presenting its face of unbelievable beauty. All you have to do is look with open eyes and receive. The world asks of you nothing impossible. Everything you desire is within you. You need not go across vast deserts or the tossing waves of storm swept oceans. The smell of new rain on dust, the scent of bluebells carpeting the woods. The glory of apples ripening. The calm of winter. Listen. The earth is asleep. Green spring, blossom, hay, birdsong, eggs, new life, everywhere.

You   Come on, then.

Cockatoo flies. The statue is silent. Dick is buying a sports car. James is smiling. Cecile has been buried. Daks is promoted to superintendent.

You close the bedroom door.

***